Outback Creed

Jonathan Macpherson

Outback Creed

Jonathan Macpherson

Chapter 1

Are you listening to me?" his father asked him, grabbing him by the shoulders. David nodded, though he hadn't been. The group of chanting demonstrators marching down the main street, flanked by cops, had captured his attention. He'd never seen such a commotion.

But his father, known locally and to David as Tracker, had his full attention now, his fearsome black eyes striking terror into the boy. He knew Tracker could tell when he lied and cringed as the expected hand struck him hard. *Whack!* on the cheek. Head jolting, left ear ringing, cheek throbbing. Eyes wide open, his throat tightened so he couldn't breathe. He wanted to buckle over and cry, but to do that in public would embarrass Tracker and only bring more of the same. So he did his best to stand upright, looking at the ground as tears streamed to the end of his nose.

"Don't miss," Tracker said. "If you do, you owe me fifty bucks. You got it?"

David nodded, still facing the ground. Finally, his

throat loosened, and he was able to suck in a breath.

"Focus! I'll meet you back in the park soon," Tracker said, then walked away.

David composed himself, wiped his face and looked up to see Tracker already lurking among the crowd of onlookers, searching for a suitable victim. But the crowd was mostly made up of locals; David could tell by the way they were dressed. Locals were too much trouble. Tracker wanted a tourist, and wandered off the path onto the long stretch of lawn that separated the street from the beach. Dozens of people lingered there, many watching the demonstration, others just enjoying the sun. Most of them wore fashionable beachwear, definitely tourists, and David tried to guess which unlucky mug Tracker was going to choose.

An attractive couple were smooching on a bench, oblivious to their surroundings. *Easy, but too young. Not cashed-up.* Then there was the group of young surfers. *Too fit; probably fast runners.* A young father and two young kids were seated around a table having lunch, the father wiping food from the little girl's chin. *Promising; the father won't leave his kids. But he doesn't look like the kind of fella to have a thick wallet.* A grey-haired couple were enjoying a glass of wine and packed lunch at a portable picnic table. *Probably retired. Grey nomads. They'll be loaded for sure.*

As the demonstration moved further along the street, Tracker circled behind the grey nomads, signalling to David with a subtle nod of the head. David nodded back, confirming. A quick look back at the cops, who had moved along with the protesters, and David headed towards the old couple. Tracker stopped just behind them, reached down to the grass and appeared to pick up a fifty-dollar bill.

"Excuse me," he said. The couple turned and saw him holding up the note. "I think you dropped this," Tracker said.

"Oh, goodness," the woman said. The man pulled his wallet from his pocket.

David took a deep breath.

"Thank you, that's very kind of you," the man said and took the fifty. That was David's cue and he bolted. The old guy stuffed the fifty inside his wallet. Before he could slide it back into his pocket, it was snatched out of his hand as David shot through.

"Hey!" Tracker yelled. "Get back here!"

David didn't look back.

"Grab that Aboriginal kid!" the old guy called.

David weaved through the kerbside crowd, caught up with the chanting protesters, zigzagging and ducking, barely noticed as he brushed past them.

He emerged on the other side of the street and sauntered down a laneway, eyes to the ground, throwing quick looks over his shoulder to make sure he was in the clear. His face was hot, his legs primed with adrenaline. He wanted to keep running, but he played it cool, focusing on the wallet in his pocket. It was soft, made of expensive leather and thick-packed to the brim. Had to be a few hundred bucks in there, at least. Tracker would be pleased.

Several streets and turns later, he arrived at a deserted park, a playground in the middle of it. He sat on a bench under the shade of a tree and scanned his surroundings. When he was certain there was nobody around, he pulled the wallet out of his pocket, flipped it open and checked its contents: the fifty-dollar bill Tracker had supplied, another twenty and a collection of tourist brochures. Not a great result. Still, there were three credit cards, each with the Paywave logo. Three hundred bucks right there, if Tracker used them before the old man reported them stolen.

David looked around for Tracker. No sign of him yet.

Then he noticed a huge beast of a dog at the far end of the park, trotting towards him. The hair on his arms stood up. David had seen this kind of dog before. Local farmers called them pig dogs and used them to hunt and kill deadly feral pigs with razor-sharp tusks. He'd never seen one roaming solo on the streets of Creed.

Was it coming for him? He stuffed the wallet in his pocket and walked away from the bench, eyes fixed on the animal.

It changed course, keeping a line on him. He stopped, but the dog did not. David's pulse thumped behind his ears, and his stomach tightened. There was no doubt it was coming for him. As fast as he was, he knew he couldn't outrun a pig dog.

He gauged the surroundings: a few trees, bushes and the playground equipment. The dog was just a stone's throw away now.

Instinct and adrenaline kicked in, and David bolted for

the playground. He made it in a few seconds and ran straight up the slide. He got more than halfway up before he had to cling to the sides. The metal was hot from the sun, burning his hands and knees as he scrambled up. He was almost there when he heard a *whump* behind him as the dog leapt onto the slide. Jumping onto the platform at the top, about ten feet above ground, he turned to see the dog, its legs flailing, paws slipping. But it couldn't get any higher. It slipped back a little, then rolled right off the side, thumping to the ground.

"Ha! Can't do that, can ya?" David mocked, unable to mask the trembling in his voice.

The animal charged back up the slide, but didn't get far before falling off again.

"Now get out of here, ya mongrel. Go on! Piss off!"

The dog was unperturbed, circling around the play apparatus until it found a ladder, which it immediately began to climb.

"Aw, shit."

It managed to awkwardly climb a few rungs. David looked around for its owner, or for anybody who might be able to help. There was no one in sight. Then a Ford flatbed entered an adjacent street.

"Hey! Hey, over here!" he called.

But the vehicle didn't stop and soon disappeared around a corner. The dog was about halfway up when David ripped off a shoe and hurled it at the dog's head. It barely noticed. He took off his other shoe and took careful aim at the animal's eye. An eye gouge was a reliable defence against older bullies, and if he could make a direct hit, perhaps the dog would bugger off.

Wham!

But it didn't. The dog was another rung higher. If it made it up to the platform or if David went back to the ground, he would have no chance. He had to fight it from up here where it couldn't use its claws. He turned around to climb down the ladder, clutching the handrails. He took one step down, looking below at the beast. He'd have to kick it in the head with everything he had, hopefully without losing a foot. He wished he'd kept his shoes on.

The dog was clinging to the rungs, struggling to make each one but managing, eyes on David as it wrinkled its snout, flashing its white teeth, nostrils quivering. Its head trembled with a deep guttural growl.

"Go away! What have I done to you?"

The dog continued to climb and growl, and David was now terrified. He raised his knee to strike. He would drop down a few rungs, then launch his heel into the dog's head, hopefully knocking it from the ladder.

Now! Do it now!

David's throat tightened, and he struggled to breathe as panic began to overcome him. He couldn't do it. He didn't dare kick that huge, snarling demonic head.

Then he saw the flatbed coming back down the road. He rushed back to the top of the ladder.

"Come on, boy! Up here!" he said.

The dog climbed a rung, then another, gaining momentum. It scurried all the way to the top, but the boy was nowhere to be seen. The dog turned and saw David running across the park towards the street. The animal leapt from the slide and hit the ground in a sprint.

David waved frantically at the driver, but the vehicle passed him.

"Wait!" he yelled, still running. The vehicle stopped, the driver looking at David through the rearview mirror. He sprinted to the passenger door and pulled it open, then burst in, slamming the door closed and looking back to see the dog closing in fast.

"That bloody dog's after me!"

"I can see that," the driver said.

The dog leapt onto the flatbed, strutted all the way to the glass window at the back of the cab, then lay down, as if to take a nap. David didn't know what to make of it. He turned to the driver, about to speak when the guy shoved a cloth over his face. David tried to wrestle it off, but the man was strong. The rag was soaked in some awful-smelling stuff, and David, already puffing, couldn't help but inhale it. Seconds later, he was unconscious.

Chapter 2

Premier Claire Bosworth stood on the small stage facing the crowd. The air was hot and dry, and she had to squint to see the faces in the crowd on the street in front of her. Most of them were quiet, listening and watching as the group of demonstrators in the front got louder and louder. With the sun behind them, it was difficult for Claire to read their placards, but she caught sight of one of them: Bosworth = Bankruptcy!

She checked her palm card and continued speaking, her voice booming out through the speakers over the crowd as she went through the usual rhetoric, calling on the people to re-elect her party so they could finish what they had started. But the chanting and jeers got louder, overpowering her voice. Then something flew towards her from the crowd, whistling by her head. Another missile hit the podium in front of her and splattered, fragments spraying onto her sleeve. She recognised the stench of rotten egg and cringed in disgust. Her bodyguards were already swooping around and shielding her as they hurried her off stage to her senior advisor, Drake, a stern, short-haired woman with cold blue eyes that matched her suit.

"Back to the hotel," Drake said, and they escorted her into the back of the nearby limousine and whisked her away.

Chapter 3

Tom McLaren helped himself to the hotel's buffet, piling a few pancakes onto his plate and smothering them with maple syrup and crushed almonds. He didn't usually eat until lunch, but it was going to be a long day. The athletic physique that had held up so effortlessly in his twenties and thirties was just a little softer and less defined these days. He had managed to hold off a lot longer than the other lawyers he knew, certainly those at his firm, but he had no doubt that if he continued with his long hours, his appetite for booze and fine food, and his hatred for physical exercise, he was heading down the highway to middle-aged spread.

But for the moment, he was still handsome and dashing in his chinos, polo shirt and boat shoes, though he looked more like he was going yachting than heading to the outback to practice law. But he was damned if he was going to suit up again in this heat, as he had done the first day. The second day, he wore suit pants and a long-sleeved shirt, but even that had proven uncomfortable. With his plate stacked, he headed back to the table where the client,

Dawn Konnigan, had joined his colleagues. Konnigan was a powerful woman, immaculately presented in business attire. Her face lit up as he approached. Tom's smile concealed his desire to rebuke her for demanding a brunch meeting, imposing herself on the little free time they had. *What a nerve!*

Ed Hitchens, the senior partner at the firm, glanced at Tom's attire and wasn't entirely happy about it, though he wasn't about to complain. Konnigan could barely take her eyes off Tom. If she was happy, Ed was happy.

Anthony, the young associate, looked at Tom with envy. He was already sweating in his suit.

"Not even a blazer?" Konnigan asked, a smile on her face.

"You wouldn't want me to sweat, would you?"

"I wouldn't mind," she said, still smiling.

"Nobody trusts a sweaty lawyer," Tom said.

Anthony loosened his tie and wiped the sweat from his forehead. As Tom tucked into his pancakes, he caught Konnigan's bodyguard looking at him and acknowledged him with a nod. Rooke nodded back and quickly averted his eyes. Tom knew that one of the most important assets of a bodyguard was size; the bigger the bodyguard, the more intimidating and deterring. Yet Rooke was lean and of average height, and Tom figured he must be incredibly dangerous and capable to get away with such an unimposing physique.

"Morning, Heinrich," Konnigan said, and they all turned to see a gangly, middle-aged guy approaching. He stood between her and Tom, wearing the briefest of swimwear, which seemed to be vacuum-sealed around his genitals. As she introduced him to the team, he turned and gave them a frontal assault.

"So, how are the negotiations going with the natives?" Heinrich asked, facing Tom.

"You mean the local Aboriginal people? Fine, thanks," Tom said, focusing on his food.

"We're hoping to wrap it up today," Konnigan said.

"Good," Heinrich said. "Seems to be taking a long time, ya? I mean, how long can you sit in a room talking?" The man's arrogance took Tom by surprise. "I suppose you know what you're doing, don't you?" Heinrich said.

"I'm trying to eat, but I'm starting to lose my appetite. Why don't you go put some clothes on," Tom said. Ed cringed, wishing Tom had been more diplomatic.

"Tom," Konnigan said, a hint of warning in her voice, "Heinrich owns power plants all over Europe. He'll be one of my biggest clients."

"Assuming we make a deal," Tom said.

"You think you can't make a deal?" Heinrich asked. "Are the Aborigines resisting?"

"It's not an invasion, Heinie," Tom said.

"I have some excellent lawyers," Heinrich said to Konnigan, dismissing Tom's remark. "They're world class. They handle these kinds of cases all the time."

"Tom's just kidding around. He's taken more land from the natives than Captain Cook!"

"Okay, funny, that's very good. Okay, so I see you all

later at the bar then, ya?" Heinrich said.

"You bet," Konnigan said. Heinrich smiled at Ed and Anthony and left. Konnigan finished her glass of whiskey and held it out to be refilled.

"I think the world of you, Tom, but don't insult my clients."

"Don't bring your clients to our meetings, especially middle-aged men in budgie-smugglers," he said.

"Budgie-smugglers?" Konnigan asked.

"Speedos," Anthony said.

"Oh. Point taken," she said.

"With no manners," Tom added.

"All right, all right," she said. "Where's the bloody waitress?" She waved at the waitress, who came over and refilled her glass.

"You'll join me, won't you, Tom? Your colleagues are a bit soft."

"I don't think it would be in your best interests for us to join you," Ed said.

"I'll have a cider," Tom said. The waitress nodded and walked away.

Konnigan turned to Rooke. He came forward and placed a briefcase on the table, pulled out three dossiers and handed them to the lawyers.

"Rooke's done a little research which may give you an edge," she said.

Tom, Anthony and Ed flicked through the dossiers on the three Aboriginal men they had been in discussion with over the past two days. Each dossier contained detailed information, complete with mugshots. One of them was Tracker Jackson. Tom's eyes widened in disbelief as he skimmed over Tracker's past criminal convictions, misdemeanors, credit history, medical history and social behaviours, even his preferred foods, beverages and sleeping arrangements. But it didn't stop there: similar information was listed about his deceased wife and son.

"It could be the difference between winning and losing. There's a bonus for each of you, if you close the deal today," Konnigan said.

Now it was obvious to Tom that Rooke's skills went beyond protection; he was clearly an expert in uncovering privileged information and gifted in the fields of persuasion, coercion and corruption: covert skills usually associated with government intelligence agencies.

Of course there was the possibility that the dossiers were purely fictional, that Rooke had made the information up, wholly or partly. He glanced at Rooke and noticed the man was staring straight ahead, like a soldier on duty, and he had no doubt the information was as reliable as its procurement was unethical.

There was commotion at the front entrance nearby as the Premier and her entourage entered the hotel. Tom watched Claire Bosworth, her pretty face looking forlorn as she was escorted into an elevator, surrounded by bodyguards who, unlike Rooke, were bulky and physically intimidating. Tom caught a glimpse of Bosworth's legs, firm and perfectly shaped, just before the elevator doors closed.

“Excuse me,” Tom said and wiped his face with a napkin.

“Where are you going?” said Konnigan.

“Is there anything else?” Tom asked.

“No,” Konnigan said.

“Then I’ll see you out there,” Tom said, and walked away.

***

Tom pressed the button to the top floor. The doors closed and he felt the lift ascending. He looked almost nervous when it stopped, and as the doors opened, he peered out and saw the entourage escorting Claire to her room, then separating and heading into different rooms. Tom pushed the button and the doors closed; the elevator didn’t move. He waited for about a minute, then opened the doors and peered out again. There was a lone security guard standing outside Claire’s door. Tom walked towards him and smiled as the man looked him over.

“Guest relations,” Tom said. “I’m here to check on Ms. Bosworth.”

“Show me some ID.”

“She’s expecting me.”

“I don’t think so. Turn around and walk.”

“Can you at least tell her I’m here?”

“Now!” the guy said, frowning. Tom opened his mouth to protest, and the guy grabbed his shoulder, just as the door opened.

Claire Bosworth set one slippered foot outside the door

and peeked out, wearing a bathrobe.

"Sorry for the disturbance, ma'am, I'm just removing this gentleman," the guard said.

"No need for that," she said, and the guard released him. She locked eyes with Tom for a long moment, and he smiled slightly. "Step aside, please," she said. The guard obeyed her, and she stepped back inside the door, disappearing. Tom cleared his throat and walked past the guard, following her inside.

***

She stood by the bedside table, her back to him as he closed the door. "What are you doing here?" she asked.

"I was just asking myself the same question," Tom said, approaching. "I've got a very big day today, and I need to be sharp," he said, stepping right behind her.

"Sharper than you were with my security guard?" she said.

"I'm standing here, aren't I?"

"Is that all you're going to do? Stand there?"

He slid his arms around her waist, loosened the belt of her robe and slid it open, the soft fabric sending tingles all over her. She turned and he moved closer, their lips meeting in a kiss that continued as they fell onto the bed.

Outside, the bodyguard turned his ear to the door, certain he had heard a muffled cry. He clenched the door handle but then heard what could only be a female groan of pleasure, and removed his hand. He adjusted his earpiece, trying to block out the sounds of his employer as she made love to the lucky son of a bitch who got past him.

***

Sitting on the edge of the bed, Tom buttoned up his shirt and put his shoes on. Claire lay on her side, eyes closed as she tried to make the most of the tingling afterglow, a welcome distraction from the humiliation she had suffered in front of the protesters. She knew it was going to be a tough gig, but hadn't anticipated such intense angst. Claire was as thick-skinned as any politician she knew and was accustomed to wearing a brave face. But seeing the disgust and hatred on the faces in the crowd was so painful she had felt nauseous.

Good thing she had coordinated her trip to coincide with Tom's meeting with the local Aboriginal people. The two had been lovers little more than a month, and the excitement was very real. Some of that excitement came from the secrecy of their affair: he had agreed to keep it out of the public eye. That meant secret rendezvous, often with Tom standing alone on the corner of an inner-city laneway in his suit, waiting to be picked up by a limo and escorted to her apartment. At this stage, only her driver knew about Tom.

Not that Tom minded. He had been widowed for almost a year and a half when he met Claire, and while he wasn't ready for an emotional commitment, he was more than ready for a physical relationship. The clandestine aspect was entirely new to him, and he had enjoyed it. Though tonight, for the first time, the novelty was beginning to wear off: being manhandled by Claire's security guard was far from exciting, and he wondered if this was going to be more trouble than it was worth.

"I could get used to sex for breakfast," Claire said.

"Sexfast," he said, in his best TV commercial voice, "the perfect way to start your day."

"Hopefully we'll have the perfect end tonight," Claire said, lying half-covered by the bed sheet.

"I've got the camping trip," he said.

"You're kidding, Tom."

"I told you about this."

"Do you know what a major operation it was to come here?"

"Come on, you would've come whether I was here or not," he said.

"Yes, but I went to considerable trouble to schedule—"

"I'm sorry, Claire, I can't. You know, you've got the better deal, here. I'm the one sneaking around hotel corridors," he said.

Fully dressed, he lay beside her and leant forward to kiss her mouth. She gave him her cheek.

"Let me know how it all goes," she said.

"Will do," he said, and got up to leave.

Chapter 4

The Land Cruiser barreled along the highway through a landscape of incredible rock formations and rich, earthy colours, contrasted with patches of brilliant white wild flowers and the intense blue, cloudless sky. Ed was behind the wheel, taking it all in. Tom sat beside him, Anthony in the back seat, both studying the dossiers that Rooke had supplied. Tom flicked through the pages of Tracker's dossier, then back to the mugshot. The man had an intimidating face, and even more so in person, as Tom had found over the past two days.

"Christ, where did they get this?" Anthony asked.

"Not on Wikipedia, that's for sure," Tom said.

"I mean, you'd have to bribe people to get this kind of info," Anthony said, looking at Tom for a reaction, but getting none. "Do you think Rooke has investigated us?"

"No doubt he has," Ed said, "and the fact that Konnigan hired us is a great compliment. You should feel good about it."

"Yeah, like you had an unsolicited prostate exam and

you got the thumbs up," Tom said, giving Anthony the thumbs up sign.

"Don't listen to him," said Ed. "This kind of practice is not unusual when you're dealing with high profile companies. The higher the stakes, the greater the need for security."

Anthony frowned and continued reading. He had a lot to learn and he knew it. He had chosen a commercial law major not only for the money, but because it had seemed to be the noblest branch of law. No ambulance chasing, no representing murderers and lowlifes and fighting for their freedom. Drawing up legal contracts between companies seemed to be an honourable occupation, and so far that had proven to be the case. But now, for the first time, he was beginning to sense there was a murky side.

Tom glanced out the window and noticed an incredible boab tree not far from the roadside. Its trunk was swollen, like it had swallowed an elephant, the top funnelling into a bottleneck. He had heard about such trees, some with hollowed out trunks that had been used to house Aboriginal prisoners in early colonial times.

He looked back at the dossier, at the photo of the Aboriginal man named Abe clipped to the front page. It was the face of a man who had known plenty of hardship and so far, he had expressed no interest in financial gain. Tom would have to find some way to appeal to him, to convince him to give up his land to QPEC, or Q-Pec, as it was commonly known, Konnigan's company. Money was not the answer. At least not on its own.

Chapter 5

Inside the outback school hall, Tom, Ed and Konnigan sat at a fold-out table, watching as Anthony gave his digital slide presentation to the three Aboriginal Elders. Tracker Jackson, still in his forties, was considerably younger than Abe and William. They listened as Anthony did his very best to convince them that their community would be better off taking QPEC's money and relocating to the proposed QPEC Community Centre, only a couple of hours away. They watched the computer-generated images of the fully equipped village, complete with a medical facility and Olympic-sized swimming pool, where they were promised they could live comfortably with financial security for generations to come.

As Anthony wrapped up, Tom noticed Ed looking hopefully at Konnigan, trying to reassure her. Tom didn't feel so optimistic. He activated the video camera on his phone and set it on the desk, aimed at the Elders, who conversed in their own language.

Abe, the most senior of the group, nodded to his

companions and turned to the lawyers. “It’s all very nice, but no thanks,” Abe said.

“But thank you for the picture show,” William said.

“Excuse me,” Anthony interrupted, “but the benefits of relocating far outweigh—”

“Are you deaf, mate?” William interrupted. “We’re not moving.”

Anthony glanced at Tom, who waved him over. He took a seat and as the Elders got up to leave, Tom took the floor.

“You’re free to stay, gentlemen. Free to watch more of your young people die, like William’s grandson, Ricky.”

The Elders stopped, all eyes on Tom.

“That tragedy could have been avoided if you weren’t two hours from the nearest hospital,” Tom said.

“Well,” Abe said, taken aback, “if they hadn’t closed the old medical centre, he’d still be here.”

“There are kids with serious health problems here in your community; there’s petrol sniffing, alcoholism. If you don’t relocate, more of your children will die,” Tom said.

The Elders chatted in the local language, the tone quickly erupting into a fierce argument: murderous looks, saliva spraying, hands waving violently in accusation. Tom stepped back and headed towards his team, greeted by a subtle smile from Konnigan.

***

Outside the community centre, Rooke stood by the Mercedes sedan, kicking an Australian football with a couple of the local kids, watching as a young journalist nearby addressed a video camera, operated by a young man.

". . . with youth unemployment at over sixty percent, this community is doing it tough. If that's not bad enough, the local garbage service hasn't collected waste from here in over a month, and won't offer any explanation to locals. When I contacted the local council, they refused to comment. Ironically, this community sits on the world's largest uranium deposit, worth billions of dollars, and mining giant QPEC is zeroing in. It's no surprise . . ." she was suddenly distracted, ". . . go, Russell, go!" she yelled at her camera operator, who swung around, capturing Konnigan, Tom, Ed and Anthony leaving the school hall. She hustled closer and got the microphone in front of Konnigan's face as Russell did the same with the camera, but only for a split second before Rooke grabbed hold of it. Russell tried to shake it free, but was no match for the bodyguard.

"Let go!" Hannah yelled, but Rooke held tight until Konnigan was inside the back of the Mercedes. He then pulled it away from Russell and tossed it on the ground. "Asshole!" Hannah said, echoing Tom's thoughts, as Rooke climbed behind the wheel. Russell grabbed the camera, but by the time he had it in position, the Mercedes was tearing down the street. Hannah set her sights on Tom, Ed and Anthony, who were heading for their vehicle.

"Have you made an offer to the—"

"We'll disclose all relevant information to the press at the conclusion of negotiations," Tom said.

Hannah signalled for Russell to stop filming, and he lowered the camera. "Look," she said, "when you do reach an agreement, think you could call us first?"

"You want an exclusive?" Tom said, as Anthony and Ed got into the vehicle.

"We've been out here for days, I think we deserve it," she said.

He stopped and looked at her. She was young and ambitious, and looked miserable. "Got a card?"

She fumbled through her handbag, pulling out a card and handing it to him.

"I'll call you when we have something to say," he said, as Ed started the engine.

"Thank you."

"In the meantime, stop shoving the camera in our faces. Deal?"

"Yes, absolutely. Thanks," she said.

"Terrific," he said and climbed into the vehicle, pocketing the card as they took off.

***

With Ed still behind the wheel, Tom riding shotgun and Anthony in the back, the Toyota journeyed deep into the breathtaking Kimberley landscape, scattered with massive rock formations, patches of thick, green bush, and vast open spaces. Ed and Anthony had swapped their suits for casual clothes, while Tom stuck with the chinos, polo shirt and boat shoes. Ed had seen beautiful pictures of the Kimberley region, but this was far more spectacular than any photograph.

His colleagues didn't seem to share his sense of wonder. Tom was holding his phone up so Anthony could see and listen to the video footage of the Elders arguing.

"I don't know, we'd have to get it translated," Anthony said.

"I don't need a translator to tell me Tracker was clearly against the old man. He was keen for a deal."

"Forget about work and take in this scenery! This will all be off limits once QPEC gets a hold of it," Ed said.

"You mean *if* they get a hold of it," Anthony said.

"Konnigan's lined up the Germans, the Chinese. Then there's the fifty million dollar advance payment to the government, government royalties. It'll happen."

"So it'll happen," Anthony said, "but nobody's told the locals yet."

"They'll come round," Ed said, "they'll come round."

***

The Land Cruiser was parked by a riverbank, with a dual compartment tent pitched nearby. Ed and Tom sat back in deck chairs, sipping beers and taking in the stunning views of a huge cliff, waterfalls and lush bush land. Anthony stepped out of the tent in sports gear, and started stretching his legs.

"You're not seriously going running?" Ed said.

"You guys ought to stretch your legs, too, don't want deep vein thrombosis," Anthony said.

"My deep vein is just fine," said Tom. "We're gonna sit back, rehydrate and take in the awe of this majestic setting."

"Save a beer for me," Anthony said.

"Sure thing," Tom said.

Anthony set off running along the water's edge.

"I'd give anything to be able to run like that again," Ed said.

"You've forgotten how painful it is," Tom said.

"There's a lot to be said for being fit."

"Such as?"

"Longevity, for one."

"Fitness doesn't guarantee a long life."

"Energy, vitality," Ed said.

"Caffeine. Vitamins. Alcohol."

"Being slim and attractive."

"Vanity? Denying yourself all life's delicacies? Where's the fun in that?"

"So it's all about fun?"

"It's about enjoying life, isn't it? For me it is, anyway," Tom said. "If I do something, it's got to be enjoyable, or at least comfortable. And if it's not, there'd better be plenty of money in it."

"To fund further enjoyment?"

"Exactly. Cheers," Tom said, and raised his beer.

"Cheers," Ed said, clinking his against Tom's. "Well, Jesus, would you look at that. It'll be toxic wasteland in a year. What a crime."

"It's no crime. Immoral, maybe. But not a crime," Tom said, and sipped his beer.

"Let's get that barbecue started," Ed said.

***

Anthony jogged between the riverbank and a rocky hillside, the campsite a few hundred yards behind him. He heard an odd sound and slowed to a halt, then stood perfectly still and stopped breathing, listening. All around him, the air was filled with an intense mix of natural sounds, mostly birds and insects. But then he heard it again: the soft, unmistakable cry of a child.

He walked over to the rocks and saw a narrow opening to a cave. The crying seemed to be coming from within.

"Is somebody there?" he said.

A savage barking sounded above him, and Anthony backed away. The pig dog stood on the rocks a few feet above the cave mouth, teeth gnashing, muscles taut and trembling in rage.

"I'm in here!" the child called.

"What's your name?"

"David."

"Don't worry, David, we'll get you out of there. Are you hurt?"

The dog leapt down onto the ground and circled behind Anthony, cornering him. It was a fearsome sight, rippling muscles and intense black eyes. A long, heavy stick lay on the ground nearby, and Anthony slowly reached for it. He held it up towards the dog and its snarling grew louder, deeper.

"Better put that down," a voice said.

Anthony looked behind him and saw the man on the

rocks where the animal had leapt from, a rifle in his hands. Anthony dropped the stick.

Bateman, the man who had abducted David by the children's playground, was in his late twenties, clean-shaven and solid.

Bateman shook his head in disbelief at his bad luck. What were the odds of running into someone out here, deep in an Aboriginal reserve, off limits to tourists? He thought about killing the young bloke, one bullet to the head. But there were others. Perhaps they would foolishly come running to investigate, and he could pick them off too. Getting rid of the bodies out here wouldn't be a problem. But three missing people would result in a massive manhunt, and that was the last thing he needed. He wasn't quite sure what to do.

***

The steaks sizzled on the barbecue. Tom, Ed and Anthony sat on the deck chairs under the supervision of the bristling dog as the gunman inspected their camp. Sitting perfectly still, Tom wondered who this man was, what he wanted and whether they could negotiate their way out of this. Twenty years of corporate law had taught him to resolve seemingly impossible situations. Of course, it wasn't every day he was held hostage, but still, there had to be a way to negotiate, he thought. If they remained calm.

He turned to Ed, who was a picture of fear and anxiety. Beside him, Anthony looked alarmed but in control. *Don't expect any help from Ed,* Tom thought. *If and when this escalates, Anthony is the one to call on.*

"Who's got the keys?" Bateman said.

Ed reached into his pocket and the dog snarled. Tom wondered if the man simply wanted to steal the car. He hoped that was true, but doubted it.

Ed handed them over, and Bateman took a phone from his belt and walked towards the river, his back to them. The dog remained on guard as Bateman, just out of earshot, made a phone call.

If he wanted the car or money, Tom thought, *he would've taken it already. What else could he want? He wasn't all the way out here, in one of the most isolated parts of the country, hoping to snare some campers. No. He was involved in some criminal activity; something lucrative, probably narcotics, and Anthony must have happened upon it. He's on the phone to an accomplice or a superior, finding out what to do next. He wants to know if he should kill us.*

Tom slowly pulled the phone from his pocket, the dog snarling at him.

"There's no coverage out here, I tried earlier," Anthony whispered. "He must have a satellite phone."

"Put it away, for God's sake," Ed said.

"Quiet," Tom said, persisting. He pressed a few buttons in quick succession, then looked at the thick surrounding bush, mentally measuring the distance from the campsite. He stood up and the dog snarled, baring its teeth.

"Tom, please!" Ed said.

Bateman had the phone to his ear. "I don't fucking care! Get out here now!" he said, louder than he intended.

He turned back to his prisoners and noticed Tom was on his feet for a moment, before quickly sitting back down. *The fool must have contemplated running,* Bateman thought, as he walked back towards them. He didn't even bother issuing another warning. If they chose to run, that would make his choice easy. He'd let the dog kill them, and would be justified in doing so.

"We'll have to wait for my acquaintance," Bateman said. "In the meantime, enjoy your barbecue. Go on!"

The lawyers got up and, with some hesitation, walked by the .dog to the barbecue, where the steaks were just beginning to char. Tom watched as Ed, tongs trembling in his hands, pulled a steak from the grill. Tom took his cutlery and noted the rounded end of his knife. He wondered if Ed had packed anything sharper and looked inside the picnic basket, where a good-sized carving knife lay. But Bateman was watching, rifle in his hands. Tom leant down and grabbed a handful of napkins.

"Care to join us?" Ed said. "There's plenty of food."

"No, I don't eat my fellow creatures," Bateman said.

"That's reassuring."

"How about a beer?" Tom said.

"Just talk among yourselves," Bateman said.

The three were soon seated and eating their lunch while the dog stood guard nearby. Tom kept one eye on Bateman, who was scratching a badly chafed and scabbed forearm as he paced back and forth; behaviour Tom knew was common among users of crystal methamphetamine. And like most users, this guy looked unstable, intense and totally unpredictable. Not the kind of guy to listen to reason or negotiate.

Bateman stopped pacing and listened.

"This is great steak, Ed," Tom said.

"Quiet!" Bateman said. They all sat still and listened as he scanned the bush behind them. Somewhere deep in the bush, people were talking. "Friends of yours?" Bateman said.

"No, it's just the three of us," Ed said.

Bateman clicked his fingers, and the dog bounced up on all fours, guarding the lawyers.

"Keep quiet," Bateman said.

"No problem," Ed said.

Bateman jogged away from the camp and stopped by the edge of the bush, listening. The distant voices continued, though what they were saying wasn't clear.

Tom kept his eyes on Bateman, who waited a moment longer, then ran into the bush.

"Spare keys under the mat?" Tom asked.

"What?" Ed said.

"Driver's side, right?"

Ed nodded.

"Get ready to move," Tom said.

"Be sensible, Tom!"

Tom looked at Anthony, raising his eyebrows, wanting to know if Anthony was up for whatever was going to go down. Anthony nodded.

Tom tossed his steak on the ground beside the dog. It swung its head in his direction, baring its teeth in warning.

Then it turned back to the steak. Tom took hold of the carving knife. The dog looked back at Tom, then at the steak. The smell was impossible for the animal to resist, and it gorged itself on the juicy meat.

Tom bolted for the tent. The dog dropped the steak and set after him with a savage growl.

"Jesus!" Ed said.

Tom ducked into the first compartment of the tent and then into the second, where he turned, grabbed the zipper of the door flap and swung it to the floor, closing it. The dog's head crashed against the thin, taut canvas. Tom fell backwards on his rear as the frenzied claws streaked down the other side of the flap, nearly piercing it, the dog going berserk.

***

Bateman was working his way through thick bush when he stopped, alarmed by the distant sound of the dog in all-out attack mode. *They can't go anywhere. If they run, they'll be torn to shreds.* The voices were not far now. He had to deal with them first, the campers later.

***

Anthony set off at a sprint towards the river, towards the child.

Ed gripped his forehead in panic and dismay.

"Lock the dog in, Anthony! Lock it in!" Tom yelled from inside the tent, not realising Anthony had left.

Ed got to his feet and peered inside the tent, where he

saw the ferocious animal on its hind legs, hacking at the door flap, beginning to make streaks in it. Ed's heart thumped in his chest, eyes blinking rapidly as he walked closer. Hands shaking, he took hold of the zipper on the tent entrance and pulled it down, locking the animal inside the tent. The dog was in such a frenzy it didn't even notice.

Tom thrust the carving knife into the back wall of the tent, making a hole. Behind him, the dog tore a long streak in the door flap, wide enough for it to get its snout through.

Tom leaned into the knife and cut a horizontal line into the canvas wall as the dog nuzzled its head through the hole in the door flap. Tom hacked away, gritting his teeth as he ripped it wide enough for his shoulders. He dropped the knife and squeezed through the tight opening, hands and head first, tearing the hole wider as he leaned out onto the ground. Ed took Tom's hand and pulled, as the dog shredded the inner door flap. Tom thrashed his way through, getting his thighs out. His right leg was all the way through as the dog burst through the inner door flap. The crazed animal pounced towards his left leg as he pulled it out, the jaws gnashing the rubber sole of his shoe.

The dog thrust its head through the hole, and Tom sprung to his feet and knocked the tent pole down, collapsing the rear compartment on top of the animal. As it bounced around inside the tent, Tom took the gas bottle from the barbecue. He charged at the tent, with the dog floundering inside. Tom held the gas bottle up, edging closer to the furious dog. He aimed for what he hoped was its head and swung the gas bottle, connecting with a thud. The animal dropped and lay motionless.

"Where's Anthony?"

"He said there was a child, he's gone after a child."

***

Bateman closed in on the voices, which were arguing fiercely in what he now recognised was the local Aboriginal dialect. He peered around a bush and saw that the voices were coming from a mobile phone that looked like it had been tossed into the scrub. On the screen played the video of the Elders arguing. Bateman realised he had been fooled. Before he could react, he heard the sound of the Land Cruiser engine starting.

***

Tom was behind the wheel, Ed riding shotgun as they sped towards the rocks, where Anthony stood with the Aboriginal child in his arms. Tom hit the brakes, and Anthony bundled David, hands tied, into the vehicle. Anthony untied David as they tore away from the campsite onto a dirt road.

"Everyone okay?" Tom asked, foot firm on the accelerator.

"Yes," said Ed, "I think we're all okay. My God." Ed leant against the side window, his chest heaving. He swallowed hard and tried to catch his breath. Then he noticed rapid movement in the bush to the side of the dirt road ahead—something ploughing through, charging towards the road. He tried to speak but couldn't, and instead turned to Tom, pointing ahead. Tom had already seen it.

"Hold on!" Tom said, as the Ford pickup burst out of the scrub, Bateman behind the wheel. It was heading towards the road in front to cut them off, or T-bone them. Tom slammed his foot to the floor, and the Toyota accelerated with a roar. The two vehicles were on a ninety-degree collision course. Tom could see where the point of impact would be and thought he might just be able to get past it in time. Teeth clenched, he glared ahead, the Ford looming large in his peripheral vision. The bumpy ground on the roadside impeded the Ford slightly, and the Toyota rushed over the point of impact, the bull bar of the Ford clipping and smashing its tail light, nudging it violently off course. But Tom was able to adjust, and charged ahead.

Bateman swung behind the Toyota and began to gain on it as the vehicles bounced over the uneven dirt road. The Ford had been modified and was lighter and faster, and he took it onto the rough roadside and began to overtake.

Tom saw the bottleneck up ahead, where the road cut into a rocky hill on the left side. On the right side was a perilous slope, scattered with trees and rocks. The road was only wide enough for one vehicle.

He grimaced as he hit top speed, the vehicles drawing nearer to the bottleneck. Bateman edged the Ford in front, and Tom knew he was either going to be cut off or forced over the slope. He decided to take offensive action and pulled the wheel to the left, ramming the side of the lighter vehicle, crunching it into the rocks.

But the impact sent the Land Cruiser into a spin, then hurtling over the embankment on its side, airbags deploying violently. Tom and his passengers watched helplessly as their vehicle slid through the red earth in a cloud of dust and rocks, glass shattering, metal crumpling. It rolled a couple of times, then came to a halt on its side.

There were groans as the airbags deflated; Tom's head was spinning. He lay on his side, his shoulder pressed against the driver's door, the red earth just a couple of inches away through the shattered window, the collapsed ceiling above even closer. He inspected himself: a few bruises and cuts but no major damage. He looked up to see Ed, suspended by his seat belt, moaning in pain. The airbag had broken his nose, and the skin beneath his eyes began to swell and turn black and blue. Anthony and the child were safely buckled up in the back.

"You've got a broken nose," Tom said. "Apart from that, are you okay?"

Ed nodded.

"Anthony?"

"We're all right," Anthony said.

"Can you get a door open?" Tom asked. Ed and Anthony tried their doors, which were facing skyward. But both of the mangled doors were jammed shut.

The front end of the Ford hung over the edge of the slope. Bateman grunted, his foot trapped between crumpled metal and the pedals. Straining, he used both hands to pull it free, the leg of his jeans soaked with blood.

He grabbed the rifle, then crawled out of the wreck onto the dirt, teeth gnashing. He limped to the side of the road and looked down the slope at the Toyota, lying on its side in a cloud of dust. Bateman lifted the rifle and looked through the telescopic sight, his hands shaking.

Still lying on his side, both his feet over the dashboard, Tom kicked the windscreen. He cocked his legs back to kick again when there was a *ca-rack*! of gunshot, immediately followed by a dull metal whump of the bullet hitting the undercarriage of the car.

"Oh fuck," Ed said, swearing for the first time in all the years Tom had known him.

"Are you hit?" Tom asked.

"No."

Tom looked in the back, and Anthony and David shook their heads. Tom gave the windscreen another kick, tearing out a corner.

Ca-rack! Another shot.

He kicked it repeatedly, the sheet of shattered glass staying in one piece as he booted it loose from the vehicle.

Bateman's hands shook uncontrollably and he fired again, hitting a tree. He groaned and lowered his rifle.

Tom climbed out of the wreckage, followed by David, who ran to the shelter of the nearby bush. Tom looked up to the road and saw Bateman climbing inside the Ford. He reached inside for Ed, who was still suspended in his seat. "Leave me!" Ed yelled. "Anthony, get the hell out!"

Anthony crawled from the back, between the console and the collapsed roof, and around the dashboard. Tom pulled him through and he raced to David's side.

Bateman turned the key and the Ford engine started. He put it into gear and jammed his good foot onto the accelerator. The engine roared but the wreck didn't move.

Clinging to the handhold, Ed released his seat belt, and his feet dropped to the driver's door. He bent down to climb through the narrow space where the windscreen used to be, but he was a lot wider than the others.

Bateman switched the Ford into four-by-four mode and planted his foot. The beat-up pickup groaned slowly forward, the left front wheel broken at the axle, picking up speed. He steered it towards the slope, towards the Toyota.

Tom could see Ed was not going to fit through the window space. He looked up to the top of the slope and saw the Ford edging its way over. Grabbing a hold of the window frame with both hands, he pulled hard, slowly prying it open. The broken shards of glass in the rubber seal cut into his fingers, and his forearms shook with the strain as the frame slowly widened.

Bateman gripped the steering wheel as the Ford toppled over the slope, bouncing and rolling straight towards the Land Cruiser below.

Anthony ran to Tom's side, and together they strained and pulled the frame just wide enough for Ed to squeeze through. They dragged him from the Toyota just before the Ford rammed it like a wrecking ball, the two vehicles hurtling further down the slope.

***

The dust had settled when Bateman came to. He crawled

from the overturned wreckage, rifle in hand, and limped to the pulverised Land Cruiser, wincing with each step. He peered inside, dismayed to find it empty. He sat on the ground and ripped his boot off, then peeled the bloody sock off to inspect his foot. Dark blood seeped from a deep gash on his ankle. He took a handful of sun-baked, red earth and packed it onto the wound, plugging it up. Growling in pain, he pulled his sock back on, then the boot. Bateman stood up and searched the area around the Toyota, soon finding footprints leading into the bush.

With trembling hands, Bateman pulled a plastic bag of powder from his pocket, tongued its contents and swallowed. Seconds later, his pupils dilated, and he set off running, rifle over his shoulder, the pain in his ankle gone.

***

Tom, Anthony, Ed and David—now with his hands free—made steady progress along a rocky hillside. Their clothes were already soaked through with sweat. Tom kept an eye on Ed, who was straining more than the others, his face bright red, veins bulging on his temple.

"There!" Anthony said, pointing out a car driving along a distant road in the valley below. "Come on!"

"Can't go that way," David said. "Rain's coming, unna?"

They looked skyward; not a cloud in sight. David pointed behind them to a thin line of dark cloud on the horizon.

"We got to stay on the high ground," David said, and

continued his course.

“I think we’ll make it,” Ed said.

“I’m with you,” Anthony said.

Tom looked at David as he walked away. “The kid seems to know what he’s talking about.”

“So do I,” said Ed. “I’m going to that road. Now come on, Tom!”

“There’s the other guy, the acquaintance. He’ll be searching the highway for us.”

“I’ll take my chances. The only walking I can manage is downhill,” Ed said.

Tom watched as David got further away.

“Maybe it’s better to split up,” said Tom.

“I agree. Much better odds,” said Anthony.

“Okay then, so I’ll stay with the boy,” Tom said.

They nodded in agreement. “We’ll send someone to pick you up, or vice versa,” Ed said.

Tom put a hand on Ed’s shoulder. “Good luck,” he said.

Ed nodded, shot Tom a friendly wink, then set off down the hill. Tom turned and went after David.

Chapter 6

Sweat poured down his gaunt cheeks, which were bright with bloody scratches from running through branches and scrub. He was pushing his body far too hard, beyond its capabilities, but he didn't know it. The pain receptors in his brain were numb. All he could think about was getting the kid back. *Should've killed those pricks! You're too soft! Well, not anymore. I'll kill 'em all on sight.*

The footprints he was following disappeared in thick scrub, and he stopped to survey the area. He squinted, mouth open, scraping his white, flaky tongue against his ground-down teeth. He spotted one of the men just as he disappeared over the crest of a hill.

***

David was eating wild berries when Tom finally caught up to him. David offered him some of his hoard, but Tom could barely breathe, let alone eat. He leant against a tree, panting and heaving, wanting to collapse. He looked at the kid, who studied the approaching black clouds, eating some more.

Tom rested his hands on his knees, sucking in breaths. He was just beginning to stabilise when the boy dropped the berries on the ground at Tom's feet.

"Time to go, unna?" David said, and set off running.

Tom straightened up and turned around, setting eyes on Bateman, tearing down a nearby hill at full speed, kicking up a blood red trail of dust. Tom got moving.

***

Thunder clapped overhead and the rain came pelting down. Tom lost sight of the kid as he pushed through the bush. He soon came to an expansive sandy clearing scattered with hundreds of rocks, some of them over ten feet tall; pinnacles reaching skyward like giant tombstones in an ancient cemetery. No sign of David, but Tom spotted the boy's footprints. He followed them through the maze of rocks, soon finding the boy sitting, waiting for him. The boy pointed out a gentle flood of rainwater that was forming on the dunes behind him, heading down towards them.

"Come on," he said.

They ran up the dunes and met the stream, running against the current in a zigzag through the rocks.

***

The sky darkened as Bateman followed the two sets of tracks through the red earth and stopped where the bush met the sandy maze of limestone pinnacles. He wiped the sweat from his eyes and jogged into the maze. But the footsteps disappeared in the streaming water. He stopped and scoured his surrounds. No sign of the boy or the man. He suddenly felt uncomfortable, slightly paranoid, as the eerie rocks towered over him.

He shook his head vigorously and set off in a sprint, running over the water, searching left and right.

Tom and David stood behind a rock, watching as Bateman, about half a football field away, ran haphazardly through the maze. David tugged on Tom's sleeve, and they set off again, running along a crop of rocks, hidden from Bateman's view as they re-entered the bush.

Bateman ran like a maniac among the pinnacles, weaving and lunging randomly behind some, hoping to pounce on his prey, but becoming more frustrated with each disappointment. He stopped and listened, hoping to hear them splashing through the shallow water. But all he could hear was soft, distant thunder and the relentless rain battering the wet ground all around him.

***

Tom and David stopped at the banks of a narrow, murky river, rain still coming down. David gathered some large rocks and lobbed them in the water a few feet apart, each one making a splash.

"No crocs," he said.

"You sure?"

"Yep. If there was one, he woulda gone for one of them rocks and we woulda seen him. Let's go," David said.

Tom followed David, eyeing the knee-deep water carefully as they crossed the river.

***

Ed and Anthony were plodding along the deserted road in the rain, their clothes soaked through, when Ed was overcome by a coughing fit, Anthony watching helplessly. He looked up and down the road, hoping to see the headlights of an approaching vehicle. The rain was heavy, visibility low. Ed buckled over and sat in the mud at the roadside, groaning and wheezing.

"Can I do anything for you?"

Ed shook his head. Anthony noticed shelter under an overhanging rock ledge a little further up the road.

"Let's get you out of the rain, come on." He slung Ed's arm over his shoulder and helped him through the mud, finally pulling him under cover. He sat Ed down, with the old guy clutching his chest.

"I'll get help," Anthony said. "Okay?"

Ed nodded, and fell back against the rock wall, panting as Anthony jogged away, disappearing in the rain. Ed watched as the road became covered in a gentle stream of storm water.

Chapter 7

Tom and David walked along an old dirt road as the rain eased, then finally stopped.

"What does he want with you?"

"Don't know. But my dad'll find him, don't worry."

"Think so?"

"True! My dad can track him anywhere. Through the rain. Even through fire."

"Is your dad Tracker Jack?"

"Tracker Jackson. Yep, that's him."

"So, Abe Whitaker must be your grandfather, right?"

"Yep. And when they get that bastard, they'll kill him."

They came to the end of a dirt road, to an abandoned car on the roadside that was half-submerged in the earth, like it had sunk.

"Let's have a rest," David said.

Tom nodded and peered down into the bushy valley before them. He wondered how Anthony and Ed were doing, especially Ed, who certainly wouldn't get far on foot. Then he turned back and saw David hunched over with his nose in the fuel tank of the car, taking a deep breath, inhaling whatever fumes were in the tank.

"Hey! Stop that!" Tom pulled the boy away from the car, and they glared at each other, Tom taken aback by the defiance in the child's eyes. "I don't care what you do when you get home. Right now I need you to be sharp. Okay?"

The kid turned away and started walking up a bushy hillside. Tom followed him. They walked for a long time without saying a word.

***

They came to a creek, and David stopped and searched along the muddy bank, soon finding a hole filled with brown river water. He knelt down and stuck his hand inside, feeling around.

"Ah!" he yelled, whipping out his hand like he'd been bitten by something. He went back in again and immediately jerked back, then thrust his hand deeper, up to his elbow. Whatever was in the hole didn't want to be disturbed.

"Bugger!" he said, feeling around. "You ever had yabby?" he asked.

"No."

"Big one in here," he said, then fell back, pulling out a black shelled animal with nasty claws. He tossed it at Tom, who ducked away from the crustacean. David pounced on it, taking it by the core. "There's a good resting place up here," he said, and led the way up the hillside through lush greenery and bright red and yellow flowers that hung like lanterns.

***

By nightfall they were inside a cave, sitting by a campfire, sharing the roasted yabby and some wild seeds David had collected. Tom's body ached all over, from both the crash and the seemingly endless walking.

David noticed Tom's index finger—half the nail was torn and hanging, black, blue and bloody. "What happened to your finger?"

"It happened in the crash, I guess. I only just noticed it."

"Give us a look."

Tom held his hand out and David carefully examined the finger. Without warning, he ripped the nail clean off.

"Ah!" Tom pulled his hand away, shocked at the child's audacity.

"It had to come off, unna?"

"That was for me to decide. Jesus!"

"I got one, too, look." David showed Tom his middle finger, which, sure enough, was missing a fair chunk of the nail. "But yours looks worse." David grinned.

"I'm glad you're getting a kick out of it," Tom said.

"We're going to be hurting for a while, mate," David said, laughing heartily, and Tom couldn't help smiling.

The fire crackled and they went back to eating.

"So aren't you going to lecture me about substance abuse?"

"It's a serious . . . you need professional help, I can't . . ."

“I never even did it before. True.”

“You picked a great time to start,” Tom said.

David tossed the yabby shell into the fire. “You’re going to talk Granddad into selling our land, aren’t you?”

“It doesn’t look like it at the moment.”

“You will.”

“How do you know?”

“You people always get what you want.”

“Which people?”

“You. People from your world.”

“Some people from your world want to sell. Including your dad.”

“Bullshit.”

“There’s a lot of money to be made.”

“Yep. Especially for the mining company.”

“For everyone.”

“Yeah, might as well take the cash, I suppose. If we don’t, they’ll take the land anyway and we’ll get fuck all.”

Tom glanced at David with a slightly raised eyebrow.

“I mean, we’ll get nothing,” David said. He didn’t know why, but he felt a kind of respect for Tom, like he had for the first teacher he liked back in second grade.

“You have a right to refuse. It’s a free country.”

“Yeah, right,” David said.

Tom got up and brushed his hands.

“No pissing in the cave, okay?”

“Sure.”

***

Tom was relieving himself on a bush outside the cave when he saw, far below, vehicle headlights bouncing along uneven ground, heading towards the foot of the hill. He finished up and raced back inside, kicking dirt all over the fire.

"Hey! What the hell!"

Tom led David back outside, and they peered down at the parked vehicle. The headlights turned off, and two flashlights came on and emerged from the car on opposite sides, both heading up the hill towards them.

"That's him on the left," David said. "See how he's limping?"

"No," Tom said. He couldn't see anything but the lights, which both stopped. One of them headed back to the car and climbed in; the light then switched off. The other continued up the slope.

"That him, coming up this way?" Tom asked.

"No. That's the other guy. Don't know who he is."

"Won't be long till he gets here."

"He won't find this place. No white man ever has. And even if he does," David kicked the dead leaves and sticks which covered the ground, "we'll hear him coming."

"This isn't hide-and-seek, mate. If he gets this close, we're in real trouble. We need a contingency plan."

"A what?"

"An alternative, a fallback."

"Plan B, unna?"

"Yeah, plan B."

"Okay," David said. He picked up a fallen eucalyptus

branch, still bearing leaves, and as they weaved around large rocks, he covered their tracks all the way back to the cave.

Inside, the boy took a stick from the fire and blew the charcoaled end, nurturing a small flame. He took Tom up a narrow passageway to a natural balcony, overlooking the main chamber. "We'll see him if he comes in."

"And then what'll we do? Throw a tantrum?"

"No. We piss bolt down there," David said, pointing to a dark tunnel.

"Why wait? Let's just go now."

"No. You don't want to go down there unless you have to," David said.

"Why? What's down there?"

"Lots of dark holes that lead to nothin'. Lose your step and *zzzick!* Gone."

"Okay, so we stay here for now."

"He won't find this place," David said.

They sat back against the wall and looked over the balcony's edge to the cave entrance below, saying nothing.

Before long, fatigue set in, and Tom was nodding off. He shook his head vigorously and took a deep breath. Still feeling groggy, he put his thumb between his eyebrows and massaged his forehead, a technique he had learned as a law student. He immediately felt sharper.

***

The tall, stocky man walked quietly up the hill through the bush, his flashlight pointed at the ground, a rifle over his shoulder. Every few yards, he would spot a crumpled leaf, a broken twig. He was far from an expert and couldn't be sure that he was on the right track, but something had made its way up this hill, and he'd find out what it was soon enough.

He continued for several yards but couldn't find any more indicators. To one side was a tall wall of smooth rock, unclimbable. The bush was practically impassable in every other direction. He turned and backtracked to the last crumpled leaf. He turned off his flashlight, took his rifle from his shoulder and looked through the night-vision telescopic sight. He searched the ground, studying the shrubs, following them under overhanging branches, walking around a boulder and along the wall of rock until he found what was surely the right place: the mouth of a cave. He stalked towards it, rifle ready, and peered around the corner, hugging the side of the entrance.

Inside he saw the extinguished campfire on the floor, the scraps from dinner. He surveyed the cave, finding the passageway, following it up to the balcony. There they were: the man and the child, sitting in the dark, both oblivious to his presence. He fixed his aim on the man, who had his hand held in front of his forehead, massaging it. He wanted a clean shot in the forehead and held still, waiting.

***

David looked at the silhouetted entrance. Something had changed; he couldn't make out exactly what. Then it dawned on him, and he leapt at Tom, shoving him violently to the balcony floor just as a *BANG!* filled the cave and a bullet slammed into the wall that Tom had been leaning against.

David grabbed the stick, the end still dimly glowing, as he and Tom crouched along the balcony towards the escape tunnel. David ripped his shirt off and wrapped it round the stick. As they ran down the curving tunnel, he ground the glowing end of the stick against the rock wall, making a trail of sparks which soon set the shirt alight, making a torch.

The rifleman ran across the main chamber to the passageway, flashlight on. He stormed up to the balcony and soon found the escape tunnel.

David and Tom came to a fork; the kid went down the left passage without hesitation, Tom right behind him. Then he stopped and Tom just about bowled him over.

"Wrong way!" he said, and they shuffled back and into the tunnel on the right. Tom looked back and saw the shaking light approaching fast.

They came to the end of the passage, a natural archway opening out to a dark crevasse that went straight down.

"This part's a bit tricky," David said, and fixed the torch sideways in his mouth. He turned around, standing on the edge, his back to the crevasse.

"Gimme a boost."

Tom locked his hands together, and David stepped up, holding Tom's shoulders.

"Closer to the edge," he said, and Tom inched closer.

David straightened up, hands on the archway, and leaned back slightly, out into the crevasse. He reached up for the wall above the archway, grabbed a hold and pulled himself up into another tunnel. Tom looked down over the edge—there was no sign of the bottom. He looked up at the handhold above the archway, just beyond his reach.

"Climb up the side. Use the rocks," David whispered from above. He held the dying torch over to one side, illuminating some handholds and footholds on the rock wall outside the tunnel. Tom looked back down the tunnel and saw the searching flashlight had arrived at the fork. With no alternative, he leaned out to one side and grabbed the first rock, then put his foot on another and stepped out, hanging over the crevasse. Hugging the wall, he grabbed the next rock, and then the next, slowly ascending.

The cold, smooth rocks were difficult to grab and barely wide enough to support his feet. Keeping his cheek pressed against the dank earth and rock, he tilted his head up to find the next handhold. He could see David, arm outstretched from the tunnel above, just beyond his reach. He lifted his foot, feeling blindly for the next foothold.

Then he heard the heavy footsteps arrive at the end of the passage below. Tom's left arm was stretched above his head, so he couldn't see the man's face. In the gap between his arm and the wall, he could see the man's boots on the edge of the tunnel, lit by the flashlight. They were extra large and a distinctive sandstone brown. As the man lingered, Tom held his breath and kept absolutely still. But his left hand was slowly slipping. He wanted desperately to grab the next handhold, though he didn't even know where that was, and had to fight his instincts and keep still. *Just a few more seconds.*

The boots finally retreated back into the passage, and Tom held on a moment longer, then lunged upward, grasping, but there was nothing to grasp. He felt a hand wrap around his wrist and looked up to see David. Tom peddled frantically against the wall, finding a foothold and propelling himself up, David helping him into the passage. He fell onto his chest, cheek hitting the rock floor.

Chapter 8

Having spent the night sleeping in complete darkness, David and Tom squinted as they walked around a passage into a sunlit chamber. A spring flowed up from the cave floor and streamed out through a large natural doorway in the rock wall. A wallaby skin bag hung from a rocky knob on the wall beside the spring. David took it and shook the dust off, then filled it with spring water. The tail was still intact, and he used it as a handle and slung the pouch over his shoulder.

They walked outside and stood on a ledge, overlooking a waterfall and a torrential river three hundred feet below, flanked by steep, rocky cliffs.

"Creed's that way," David said, pointing over the river. "Not far now."

"How long do you reckon it'll take?"

"Dunno. Maybe a day, if you stop dawdling," he said with a cheeky smile.

Tom smiled back, though the idea of walking a full day in the sun, eating whatever bush tucker David could find, with two sociopaths in pursuit, was unsettling. Tom turned back to the rocky hill behind them, looking it over.

"Don't worry about that bloke. He's gone. Heard him take off in his car couple of hours ago."

They set off along the ridge of the gorge with the sun at their backs, blue sky above.

To pass the time, they swapped jokes and amusing stories, and David taught Tom how to extract nuts from plants, and how to steal eggs from a bird's nest without getting his eyes poked out by an angry mother bird. He taught him how to suck the contents out of the eggs, but he couldn't teach him to keep the stuff down. Tom decided to stick to nuts and berries.

The first few hours were tougher than Tom anticipated. He carried the sack of water over his shoulder as they walked up and down rocky hills, through soft sand and tall reeds and thick, prickled scrub that cut holes in his pants and stung his limbs, while his stomach ached from hunger. But eventually, he got into a rhythm and didn't notice the pain and hunger. He barely noticed the hours passing, or the sweat pouring. When he removed his shirt and wrapped it around his head to protect him from the mid-morning sun, he noticed his torso was slimmer than it had been in years. He suspected it was mostly due to dehydration. Though he wasn't back to the athletic shape of his twenties, he looked and felt considerably better.

They came to a picturesque sandy riverbank, and David stopped, taking it in. "You keep going, I'm going to rest here a while."

"I could use a rest."

"No, you keep going."

"Have you got a can of kerosene stashed in the bushes?"

"Piss off!"

"What is it? What's wrong?"

"None of your business. Just follow the river to the highway, it'll take you to Creed."

Tom stood firm, a curious look on his face.

"I gotta drop a shit, okay? I'll catch up."

Tom nodded and set off along the bank. He walked for a quarter of an hour or so, then sat down on the riverbank, waiting for David. Something was troubling the kid and he didn't feel right leaving him. He skimmed a few stones over the water, then headed back.

He found the boy just where he had left him, lying face down, one cheek in the sand, arms outstretched like he was embracing the beach. Tom crouched beside him, patting his shoulder. "Let's go, mate." He could hear the boy faintly sobbing. "Come on, David, we've got to move. There's still a couple of nuts out there with rifles." But David didn't respond. Tom understood the child was grieving, but now was not the time.

Expecting a struggle, Tom put his arms around the boy and hauled him off the sand. He put him over his shoulder and carried him off the soft sand and along the rocky bank. David flopped about, sobbing quietly, completely consumed by sorrow. Finally, the weight became too much, and Tom set him down gently. David immediately rolled onto his side, covering his eyes.

"Look, I know how you feel, mate. Best thing to do is keep moving."

No response.

"You'll feel better, believe me. Come on," Tom said, grabbing the kid's arms and pulling him to his feet. David finally got walking, facing the ground. Before too long, he was more upright, and finally he was walking with some speed.

"My mum used to take me to the beach," he said.

"And she's gone now?"

David nodded. "You always do that in sorry time? The walking?"

"Doesn't have to be walking. I used to go swimming. I'd swim dozens of laps, till I was completely knackered. Lately, I prefer to go for a drive. But it doesn't matter what it is. As long as you keep moving."

"You lose someone too?"

"Everybody loses someone. Eventually."

"Who was it? Your wife?"

Tom considered the question for a moment, and part of him wanted to tell the boy. "I'm not going to swap sad stories with you, mate. No sense in that. Let's just keep moving."

***

They traveled for hours in the searing sun, sipping from the wallaby skin pouch, which was about half-empty by the time they got to the highway. Tom's chinos were frayed and torn, and his boat shoes looked like they'd been dragged over hot coals. The sweat stung the scratches that covered his hands and legs. In order to avoid being spotted by the two gunmen, they stayed off the highway, walking parallel to it through the boulders and scrub, sacrificing speed for safety.

Tom recognised the huge boab tree by the roadside with its unforgettably wide trunk. He had passed it before in the vehicle heading out to the Aboriginal community, only it was on the other side of the road that time.

"I know that tree," Tom said, stopping and checking his bearings. "Your town's the other way, isn't it?"

"You said you wanted to go to Creed. Not far, now."

Tom was taken aback by the boy's unselfishness. "You're a good kid, David, but you ought to put yourself first."

"You helped me, didn't you?"

"It was Anthony, my colleague, not me. Truth is, I probably would have left you there and gone to the police."

"True?" David asked.

Tom nodded. "True. You've got to put yourself first. Nobody else will."

David looked at the ground and kicked a stone out of the dirt, trying to hide his disappointment. "That's not right. Everyone's gotta help out."

"The world doesn't work that way."

"Bullshit. See this?" he said, holding up the wallaby skin pouch. "Someone left it in the cave for the next blokes: you and me. What if they just took it?"

Tom smiled, appreciating the boy's retort.

"City folks always in trouble coz they don't think about the next bloke. My people been out here for a long time.

We look out for each other. That's our, our . . ." he said, searching for the word.

"Your motto?" Tom said.

"Our creed."

"That's great, but it won't get you far."

The child looked up, straight ahead, and then smiled. "It'll get us into town. Then we're having lunch. Your shout, right?"

Tom smiled. "You got it. Whatever you want."

"You see, Tom? That's how it goes, unna?"

"Fair enough," Tom said, still smiling.

***

They dragged themselves to the pub on the edge of town and collapsed into the nearest booth. They ordered a couple of meat pies and fries, a pitcher of cola and a pint of beer. They scoffed their lunch down without saying a word.

"Best meal I've ever had," Tom said after the last mouthful. "I'll get you a proper meal later, just wanted to get something quick."

"No worries, that was grouse."

"No, I insist we go to a restaurant, once we've been to the police. You can have anything you like, then I'll get you a ride home."

"I'm not going to the coppers."

"Hey? Of course you are. We both are."

"Not me. I'll head home. Don't worry 'bout the next feed, we're square."

"We've got to report this."

"I'm not going!"

"Look, whatever problems you've got with the police, they're not going to worry about that now. They're going to be more concerned about finding my friends, and catching those two psychos out there. Believe me."

David shook his head, slurping down the last of his cola and looking around like he was about to do a runner.

"Hey," Tom said, leaning towards the boy and getting his full attention. "I need you to tell the cops so they can save my friends. If I tell the story on my own, they'll have doubts, they'll take longer to act. Meanwhile, my friends are probably walking around out there in the heat, dehydrating. They don't know how to find food or water. How long do you think they'll last? If you back me up, the cops will act faster. You remember Anthony? The guy who risked his life to get you out of that cave? Can you do it for him?"

David's eyes dropped and he nodded his head. "But you don't leave the cop shop without me. Deal?"

"Deal."

Chapter 9

Tom sat at a desk opposite two cops in the interview room. Sergeant Watson was tall and solid, his skin so weathered it was hard to tell how old he was, but Tom guessed he was about sixty. Constable Kris Somers was youthful and attractive, far easier on Tom's eyes. Despite their friendly and relaxed demeanors, both were professional and methodical, wasting no time in getting descriptions of Anthony, Ed and the gunman. They had tried to trip Tom up a couple of times, but he knew that was necessary in order to make sure he wasn't bullshitting.

"Goodo," said Watson, "I'll need to corroborate your story with the boy's version; standard procedure, you understand." Tom nodded. "But in the meantime, I'll have squad cars patrol the highway and roads, hopefully pick up your mates."

"Thank you," Tom said.

"Kris, you head the search, put the word out," Watson said.

"Will do," Kris said, and headed out the door.

"Do you need any medical attention? You probably got a concussion in that roll over," Watson said.

"No, no, I'm fine. Could I use the facilities?"

"Yeah, course." Watson led Tom into the main floor of the police station, which was sparsely furnished with some benches and a few empty desks and computers.

"Right over there," Watson said, pointing across the room. "There's tea and coffee in the lunchroom. Help yourself, mate."

Tom nodded, and as he walked towards the men's room, he glanced over to David. He was sitting behind a windowed office, being interviewed by two cops who, along with Watson, were the only ones in the building. He smiled reassuringly at the boy, and David responded with a thumbs up.

Inside the men's room, Tom washed his hands, then his sunburnt face as the fatigue began to hit him. He thumbed the pressure point above his nose, then wandered into the lunchroom, where he took up the sergeant's offer and made himself a coffee. Standing in the doorway, gazing over the workstations and sipping his coffee, something caught his eye: a screen saver on an unattended desktop computer. It was a photo of three guys, probably off-duty police officers, sitting at a bar. Something about it bothered him, and he stepped closer, but the image changed, rolling to another photo, this time of a beautiful Balinese beach. He walked a little closer, then noticed Sgt. Watson on the other side of the floor, walking towards him.

"Would you like a ride somewhere, mate?" Watson

said.

"Sure, but I'll wait for the boy," Tom said, and looked back at the computer screen.

"Goodo," said Watson, watching Tom, whose eyes were glued to the screen. Yet another photo image appeared, this time of a plate of lobster and a beer.

"Something wrong?" Watson said.

The first photograph reappeared: it featured Watson and two other guys sitting at a bar. Tom spilled some coffee, his eyes widening in horror as he recognised that one of the guys was the gunman, the guy who'd abducted David. As Watson got closer, Tom turned, about to tell him. Then Tom noticed Watson's boots: extra large and a distinctive sandstone brown—the boots he'd seen in the cave. Tom's mouth was open, but he couldn't speak.

Had he not spent a day and a half baking in the outback sun, Tom would have responded faster. But he was unable to avoid the Taser as Watson struck his chest. The electric blast sent him collapsing to the floor.

"Donna!" yelled Watson, pulling the cuffs from his belt as he crouched over Tom and grabbed his wrist. Tom rammed an elbow into Watson's jaw and broke free, staggering to his feet. He saw David looking back through the glass, terrified.

"Run, David!" Tom yelled, before he was Tasered from behind and dropped to the floor.

Sgt. Watson's daughter, Constable Donna Watson, a robust young woman, planted a knee in his back and smothered his mouth with a filthy cloth. As he drifted out of consciousness, he saw David running for the door, only to be grabbed and pinned down.

Chapter 10

Tom woke to the muffled rumbling of a car's engine, which eased to a halt, followed by the pull of a handbrake. It was dark and, lying in the fetal position, he extended a hand and felt the metal panel above him. He realised he was in the trunk of a car. A moment later, the trunk creaked open, and light streamed in behind two silhouetted figures. One of them leaned over him, and he saw the electrodes firing just before he felt the sting of the Taser on his chest.

Donna and another police officer hoisted Tom from the trunk. His entire body was taut, muscles clenched like they were cramping up. He moaned, unable to resist as they dragged him by the arms, face down over rocky ground. The woman was strong but the man seemed to be struggling.

"This way," he heard the young male officer say, and they dragged him in another direction. Tom had no doubt the officers intended to kill him. He slowly inhaled and the tension in his muscles began to ease. *Need to incapacitate them. Punch the guy in the balls. Woman in the kneecap.* But his muscles were locked up. He took another breath and he felt them loosen slightly. *One more breath.*

But he didn't get a chance. The ground below suddenly dropped a hundred feet as his face was suspended over the edge of a cliff.

"Ready?" Donna said. "One . . . two . . . three!"

As they flung him, Tom thrust himself backwards and lunged for something, *anything!* He caught a hold of the man's gun belt with both hands. The guy was short and light, and staggered close to the edge, with Tom's legs dangling over.

"Get him off me!" the guy yelled.

Tom's legs thrashed as he tried to get them back on the cliff top. The scrawny cop unclipped his gun, but before he could use it, Donna's baton came smashing down on Tom's forearms, forcing him to let go of the belt. He dropped to the cliff edge, and as he bounced over, he grabbed the man's boot with both hands, pulling his foot from under him.

They both went over, the man above him crying out in aggrieved horror as they plummeted. But Tom's fall was halted when he smacked onto flat, hard rock, watching the cop sail past him, screaming all the way to the bottom.

Tom lay still on the ledge, his ears ringing.

"Craig?" Donna called, leaning over the cliff above him, hands over her mouth as she sobbed. She was looking past him to what must have been the remains of the cop. "Craig!?"

There was no answer from the cop below.

Then she looked at Tom and her face shrivelled in rage. She pulled the gun from her belt, and as she took aim, Tom hugged the cliff wall. He felt the bullet whiz past the back of his head. She fired again, and he heard the bullet bounce off the rock wall nearby. Tom glanced over the cliff and saw the dead cop sprawled out on some rocks, several yards short of a stream. Tom knew he couldn't make it into the stream, but thought he might make it to the muddy bank. He remembered David digging through the soft mud for the yabby. Maybe this mud was just as soft, soft enough to cushion his fall and stop his bones from breaking. As the cop fired another shot, he decided it was his only chance. He bent his knees, braced his feet against the cliff wall and sprung them straight with everything he had as another shot was fired. He hurtled away from the cliff in an arc which took him over the cop and towards the stream.

He struck the muddy bank feet first like a two-pronged fork, his arms spread, stopping him from sinking beyond his chest. His head jolted forward, face buried in the soft, glorious mud. He raised his head, coughing out a mouthful of the brown muck. Another shot was fired, and he leaned forward, arms stretched, clinging and pulling himself onward. A bullet struck the mud beside his face, and he groaned, pulling his right leg up and kicking back, gaining a couple of feet. Not far from the bank was a tree with long, leafy branches stretching out from its trunk.

He trudged on, kicking, pulling, scraping until both his legs were finally on the surface. The bullets came in a flurry as the cop took less time to aim, desperate to get him before he made it to the cover of the tree. But he did make it, unscathed, and he crawled behind the trunk and collapsed onto some soft, green shrubs. The gunfire stopped and there was silence.

He waited, keeping perfectly still. Several minutes passed before he ventured away from the trunk, still hidden by the leafy branches above. He crawled to the edge of the shade and peeked up past the branches to the cliff top. He scanned the cliff top, left and right. She wasn't there. *A trap? Or is she on her way down?* He looked over to the lifeless body in the police uniform. *She'll be on her way down to finish me off and to retrieve the dead cop.*

He got to his feet and stalked over to the dead man, eyes darting back to the cliff top. Tom was surprised at how intact the body was: barely any blood, just a thin spray from the back of the head, like ketchup squeezed from a plastic bottle. He took the water bottle from the cop's belt and the mobile phone. The gun holster was empty. There was no sign of the gun, and he wasn't about to scour the surroundings looking for it while the other cop was making her way down. Tom noticed a large, folded envelope sticking out of the man's pants pocket. He tore it open to find it full of cash. He had no idea what his next move would be, or how he could return safely to civilisation, but he figured a handful of hundred-dollar bills could come in handy. He pocketed the envelope and set off along the riverbank.

Chapter 11

TWO MONTHS EARLIER . . . Konnigan was dining with Premier Claire Bosworth and Drake, Claire's senior advisor. Apart from their table and Claire's bodyguard nearby, the restaurant was empty. It was positioned in the State Parliament building, with beautiful views over the city, and was exclusive to politicians and select guests, like Konnigan. She cut into her rare steak and took a mouthful.

"It's a wonderful state, Premier, my compliments. Now tell me, what did you have in mind?" Konnigan said.

"Well, as you are aware, your proposed uranium mine has plenty of opponents. My political rival will be campaigning against it in the coming election. Then there's UNESCO, who've been pestering us about a World Heritage Listing . . ."

"Lots of people are against the mine. We're used to that," Konnigan said.

"A World Heritage Listing would put the area off limits, permanently. Unfortunately, there is a growing faction within the party that supports the listing, fearing that if we don't protect the area, we'll lose the coming election."

"Go on," said Konnigan.

"If QPEC Mining were to become a supporter, I feel certain it would unite our party, and protect your interests before the election."

"How much?"

"I beg your pardon?"

"How much?" Konnigan repeated, with more than a hint of impatience.

Claire looked at Drake, who gave her the slightest nod as she carved a slice of pork.

"Well," Claire said, "all things considered, including the significant opposition from various interest groups, some of whom I've mentioned—"

"Drop your fucking weasel words and tell me straight. How much?"

Claire stopped chewing and looked over the table to Konnigan, who, lips red from the bloody steak, stared blankly straight back at her. Claire was visibly shaken, unaccustomed to being spoken to in such a way. She took a sip of wine and looked at her plate, refusing to respond or even make further eye contact with Konnigan.

Drake whipped out a notepad and scribbled down a figure, which she handed to Konnigan. "The mining issue is divisive. This would go a long way to galvanizing our party and putting us in a strong position—"

"This mining deal is a golden fucking goose to your government. It'll get you back in black. I expected gratitude. Not extortion."

"Ms. Konnigan!" Drake said. "May I remind you—"

"Shut up. If you knew anything about me, did any kind of checks, you wouldn't insult me like this. You're like a couple of fucking hicks!"

Claire's bodyguard moved towards Konnigan, and she stood up, infuriated by the gesture. Claire dismissed the bodyguard with a subtle gesture, and he retreated.

"You'll get your money. And if that land should be world heritage listed by the UN, the federal government, or the fucking American president, I will hold you personally responsible."

The waiter appeared with a glass of whiskey on a tray. Konnigan whipped it off, took a swig, then stormed out with the glass in hand.

"Delightful lady," Claire said.

Rooke was waiting in the driver's seat of the Mercedes, parked in the shaded lot by the side of Parliament House. He saw Konnigan approaching and started the engine. She finished her whiskey and tossed the glass into the bushes before climbing into the back. Rooke put his foot down and drove out onto the road.

"Everything okay, ma'am?"

"They've got no money for their campaign, which they are going to lose. If we don't get the land before the election, we never will."

"Maybe you need to think laterally," Rooke said.

"Go on."

"The Aboriginals are comfortable where they are.

Maybe you could make them uncomfortable." She looked at him in the rearview mirror, eyes screwed up in a frown. "No offense intended, ma'am. I thought you hired me for that kind of thing."

"If this were a developing country, I wouldn't hesitate."

"I could talk to some of the cops in Creed. See what's what."

"Okay. But before you offer any kind of bait, be damned sure they'll bite."

"Of course, ma'am."

Chapter 12

"Shut the door, for Christ's sake," Sgt. Watson said softly. Constable Ryan, young and athletic, swiftly obeyed. Watson sat on the edge of his desk, arms folded, towering over Donna and Ryan. He wanted to yell at his daughter. How could she balls up something so simple? The guy was unconscious. There were two of them, both armed. This was a bloody awful mess and he was going to have to clean it up.

"We can't find him on our own, we're going to need help," Donna said.

"Have you said anything to anyone?" Watson asked.

"No," she said.

"I mean *anyone*?"

"It's just the three of us, and Bateman."

"Keep it that way," Watson said. "The guy's a cop-killer. That's how we frame it. Get the word out."

"You sure you want a manhunt? I mean, the media and all?" Ryan said.

"No media, for Christ's sake. We keep it quiet, just our guys. But we've got to get everyone on board fast."

"How's that going to work? If one of the guys brings him in, gets him on record, we'll have feds crawling all over us."

"The guy killed Craig Piper. Do you think any one of our guys is going to bring him in alive?"

"I don't know, maybe."

"All right, leave it to me, then. You get back out there and get after him. And get Bateman on the job, tell him I don't give a fuck about his ankle."

They left his office, and he closed his eyes and palmed his face, trying to gather his thoughts. His hand slid down to his mouth, eyes widening as he remembered the CCTV cameras in the station. He walked out of his office and behind the front counter, where he saw the live feed streaming through. He fidgeted with the digital video recorder, watching the monitor as he wound back footage of Tom and David being tackled and Tasered. Watson tried to delete the footage, but his technical skills were limited, and he couldn't get the machine to cooperate. Frustrated, he unplugged it and took it out the back door. A quick look; the coast was clear. He dumped it on the pavement with one end up on a step and proceeded to stomp it into a mangled, twisted mess.

"Boy, oh boy!" said Constable Kris Somers, walking around the corner of the building.

"Bloody thing's faulty."

"If it wasn't, it sure is now."

"Aren't you supposed to be on the road?"

"I was, I just came back to—"

"Never mind, I need you to get my dog."

"Your dog? What's going on?"

Chapter 13

Tom's body was caked with dry mud as he ran beneath trees along the riverbank, the mobile phone in his hand. His muscles were aching from all the running and walking he'd done since the previous morning, but he noticed his endurance and stamina had improved. No longer wheezing and gasping, he felt like he could continue jogging at a steady pace for hours. Weaving between bushes and trees, he followed the river and stopped when it became a waterfall.

He checked the phone. Still no signal. He walked to the edge of the fall and checked again. Not a bar. Wiping his brow, he looked over the edge to the river below, which cut through thick bushland. Tom turned back, looking behind him, listening. He closed his eyes and listened for telltale sounds of someone following—keys jingling, the sound of police boots crashing through foliage. But the chorus of a million insects and birds was all he could hear. He figured he must have run a couple of kilometres through bush that was impenetrable to vehicles, perhaps even off-road bikes. If anyone was going to follow him, it would have to be on foot, or by helicopter.

He looked through the treetops to the skies: clear blue, not a chopper in sight. *Would they have access to a chopper?* He couldn't be sure. It depended on how deep the corruption went, how many of the cops were involved. *Surely none of the local police were helicopter pilots?* But how the hell would he know? He'd heard of farmers up this way flying helicopters to muster cattle. Maybe the cops would use one of those farmers. *Okay, that being the case, how are they going to find me? The trees are thirty to fifty feet high!* No local cattle-mustering farmer would be equipped with the high-tech thermal imagery technology that he'd seen used on reality TV cop shows. *How do you know? You can't make assumptions about how wide this corruption goes, or what equipment is available to the local cops. All you can do is move and hopefully get a signal somewhere, if you can keep the phone battery alive long enough. Then call city cops, lawyer colleagues back home, the newspapers. Get loud and get help. Hell, call Claire, she's the Premier! She'll be able to offer some protection till you get to Perth. And if the battery dies? Get to a road and take your chances hitch-hiking. Make your way to one of the bigger towns down south.*

He climbed down the bank to the lower ground, put his wallet, the envelope of cash and the mobile phone aside, and stepped under the cool waterfall, washing the muck from his body. He took his clothes off, washing them as best he could, scraping the mud off with his fingernails, then tossed them onto the rocky riverbank. He sat down on the smooth rock directly beneath the fall, the cool, clear water washing over him, massaging his neck and the back of his head. He began to wonder about what had happened to David and was suddenly overcome with emotion, his eyes beginning to water.

A piercing scream startled him, and he looked up to see a white cockatoo perched in the branch of a tree above.

Time to move!

He stepped out from under the waterfall, rung his clothes out and pulled them back on. The cockatoo kept screaming like it was in mortal danger as he set off again along the bank, heading downstream.

Chapter 14

At the foot of the cliff, a crowd of about a dozen somber police officers watched as Constable Craig Piper's body was loaded into the back of a police van. There were a dozen squad cars and a police off-road vehicle with a horse float attached to the back.

Sgt. Watson and Donna were away from the group, standing over a handgun which lay in the mud on the riverbank.

"It's Craig's," Donna said.

Watson leaned down to pick it up.

"No," she said.

He looked at her, questioning, and she planted her boot on it and buried it deep in the mud. She pulled her foot out, and the hole above the gun mushed over, concealing it.

"Goodo," Watson said. "I'll take it from here. You go take care of the other thing."

"Go get him," she said. He nodded, and she took some comfort from the conviction in his eyes.

Another officer walked a horse to Watson's side, and he mounted the animal. He organised the officers into a skirmish line, with himself at the centre; Kris, the young constable, to his left, holding the pig dog on a leash, its nose to the ground where Tom's muddy footsteps led into the bush.

"Listen up! The suspect is armed with Craig Piper's handgun, and obviously willing to kill. Be sharp. If in doubt, shoot to kill," Watson said.

"Shoot on sight!" one of the men yelled, others voicing their agreement.

Then he leaned down towards Kris. "When we get close, he'll want to break loose," Watson said. "Wait till I give the word." She nodded. "Keep the line tight," he yelled, and they set off into the bush on Tom's trail.

Donna and Ryan stood beside a paddy wagon, watching the other officers as they disappeared into the bush.

"What did you get?" Donna asked.

"Taipan," Ryan said.

"Will it do the job?"

"Fucken oath, it will." They looked over to see a police wagon rumbling through the bush over the uneven ground towards them. Bateman was at the wheel, in uniform. He parked right beside them.

"G'day," Bateman said through the open window.

"Hey," Ryan replied. Donna didn't acknowledge him. "How's the ankle?" Ryan asked.

"Ah, it's okay." Bateman stepped out of the vehicle with a limp, his ankle heavily bandaged. "Got some good painkillers."

"I bet you do, you fuckin' junkie," Donna said and shoved him back against the vehicle. "If you weren't off your head, none of this would've happened."

"You don't know what you're talking about," Bateman said.

"I know exactly—"

"Hey, hey!" Ryan said, stepping between them. "Where is he?"

Bateman walked them around to the back of the vehicle and opened the rear doors. Inside the caged compartment was David, hands cuffed, lips bloody. Bateman grabbed his cuffs and dragged him out of the vehicle onto the ground.

"There's no need for that!" Ryan said.

***

Abe was walking along the road in the middle of the Aboriginal community, looking for his grandson. He saw a group of kids kicking a football and squinted his weary, weathered eyes. David wasn't one of them. He had promised to take the boy fishing in the morning, but neither David nor Tracker had been home. He looked down the road where another group of kids were playing, and shuffled on.

A moment later, a beat-up car pulled up beside him, and Tracker leant out the window. "David's in trouble, get in," Tracker said, urgency in his voice.

Abe climbed into the passenger side, and Tracker drove down the road and onto the highway, out of town. The vehicle rattled and shook as he took it to top speed.

"What did he do?"

"The usual. Shoplifting."

"Why weren't you looking after him?" Abe asked.

"He's a born troublemaker. Nothing I can do."

"Rubbish. He just needs a bit of time. You shacking up with what's-her-name doesn't exactly help," said Abe.

"Ah, don't start."

"The boy needs a helping hand."

"So help him," Tracker said.

"I will."

"Good."

Abe looked out the window into the bush, and neither of them said a word for several minutes. They turned off the highway onto a bush track, a dust cloud forming behind the car.

"They chase him all the way out here?" Abe asked.

"Yep."

"Hmm. Long way to run," Abe said.

They drove up the hill, then off the road to the river at the foot of the cliff, where the police cars were parked and Donna, Ryan and Bateman were waiting. No sign of David.

"Fuck!" Tracker said.

"What?"

"That copper's got it in for me. I'm not going near him."

"Okay, keep your knickers on. You stay in the car," Abe said. Tracker left the engine idling as Abe got out and approached the officers. Bateman walked towards him, heading for Tracker.

"Leave him out of it, we're just here for David," Abe said.

"Steady on, mate," Bateman said, continuing on his way.

"Granddad!" David called, sitting in the dirt with his hands cuffed around a tree.

Abe turned furiously to the cops. "You got no right to treat him like that! Let him go!"

"All in good time, love," Donna said.

"Get them cuffs off him right now!"

"We will, just need you to sign a release first," Donna said, holding out a clipboard with a pen and a document attached.

Abe looked back to see Bateman leaning into the car, talking to Tracker, then handing him a white envelope before stepping away. Without even glancing at Abe, Tracker turned the car around and drove back the way they had come. Abe's mouth fell open in utter disbelief. He wasn't sure what to make of it.

Bateman limped back towards Abe, eyeballing the old man and grinning at him. Abe swallowed hard, then looked over to his grandson. Fury began to burn inside of him.

"Okay, now sign this and we'll release the boy," Donna said.

Abe composed himself and turned back to the officers. "What's he done, anyhow?"

"Petty theft. Assault."

Abe took the clipboard and pen and she showed him where to sign. He looked at the page, full of words that he couldn't read. Then he noticed the QPEC Mining symbol on the top of the page.

"Okay, but before I release him, I want to have a word, let him know what trouble he's caused."

"Go ahead, love," she said.

Abe turned and walked over to David. He took hold of a large-leafed plant, and used it for support as he crouched beside him, speaking in his ear. "Time for you to be a man," Abe said. Then he spoke in his native tongue. "Go to the Dreaming Cave. Remember that place?" David nodded. Abe snapped off one of the large leaves and put it in David's hand. "Get out of those cuffs and get moving. No matter what happens, don't worry about me. Okay?"

David nodded. Abe tousled the boy's hair, got up and walked back to the cops. David discreetly snapped the leaf in half, a clear juice dripping out of it. He directed the flow of liquid onto his wrists beneath the cuffs. "Okay," Abe said. "Let me sign this thing." Donna handed him the clipboard and he put the pen towards the paper. But then he stopped and moaned, eyes wide open.

"Christ, he's having a heart attack!" Ryan said.

Abe collapsed to the ground, his face a picture of utter terror.

Donna crouched beside him, grabbing his hand, which still held the pen. "You've got to release the boy!" she said. She held the clipboard close and put his pen hand to the paper.

But his hand spasmed and contorted, the pen falling from his fingers. She picked it up and shoved it back as saliva ran from the sides of his mouth, his head trembling. "Sign it! Sign the fucking thing!" She pulled his taut hand to the paper, getting the pen very close. Then his arm went slack, and she unwittingly jerked it, the pen scribbling a line over the page. "Fuck!" She looked at him, his eyes closed, his body limp.

"The boy!" Bateman yelled. They looked over to see the handcuffs lying at the base of the tree.

"Fuck me!" Donna yelled. She sprung to her feet and ran into the bush, Bateman limping after her.

Donna stopped and listened, but couldn't hear anything above the sound of Bateman limping through the bush. "Stop, Bateman!" she yelled, and he did. She listened, hoping to hear the boy crashing through the bushes. She waited a long moment, then grabbed her temples as if in the throes of a massive headache. She walked back to the clearing where Ryan crouched beside the old man, fingers on his throat feeling for a pulse.

"Dead as dog shit," Ryan said.

"Well, this is just a great bloody day all round! Dad's gonna be thrilled about this!"

"Look on the bright side," Bateman said, limping into the clearing. "At least you didn't have to do him."

"Hello," Ryan said, pointing to another police car arriving at the scene. "Who's this numbat?"

"Just shut up, I'll handle it," Donna said as the car ambled over, a fresh- faced young cop at the wheel. "What are you doing here?"

"I got word about the cop-killer. Came to join the hunt."

"Bit late," Donna said. "But this old Abo needs to go to the coroner's. Heart attack."

"Bugger!" the cop said.

"We can't leave base, so if you wouldn't mind, we sure would appreciate it."

"What happened?"

"Well, he just wandered by to see what the fuss was all about, then the old fella just keeled over. Just like that."

The cop looked at Abe's lifeless body. "Just like that, eh?"

"Yeah. Just like that," Donna said, opening the rear door of the cop's squad car. Donna and Ryan lifted Abe and loaded him onto the back seat. "Really appreciate your help," Donna said.

Chapter 15

Tracker Jackson drove along the deserted highway, singing to the song on the radio in an attempt to calm himself. He was sweating, and he felt hot with panic, shocked at what he had done. *You'll be all right, just calm down. The old man was coming to the end anyway. And the boy, well, he shouldn't have been born in the first place.*

His mind wandered back to the familiar cycle of thoughts that had haunted him for years. If Tracker had not been in prison all those years ago, his wife wouldn't have been savaged by those bastards from down south. When he was released several months later, he caught up with both of them. Made them pay the price.

But his wife bore a child and, unlike Tracker, she loved David. His father may have been a rapist, but David was an innocent child. Tracker saw things differently. Still, he allowed her to have it, on the condition that they give it up for adoption. She had agreed, gave him her word. But the birth was complicated, nearly killed her. She wouldn't be able to have children again. David was to be her only child, robbing Tracker of the opportunity to have children of his own. He never forgave the boy for it. Now that the boy's mother was dead, Tracker wanted to move on with his life. David was a constant reminder of his pain and regret. With David and his grandfather gone, he could start a new family.

The flashing lights in the rearview mirror caught his eye. "Aw, piss off," he said, refusing to slow down. The squad car was soon cruising beside him, Bateman at the wheel, waving at him to pull over. He slowed and stopped on the red earth at the shoulder of the road. Bateman pulled over beside him, still on the highway.

"The boy's taken off," Bateman said.

"You're joking! How did you fuck that up?"

"Doesn't matter. You're gonna find him. Get in."

Tracker growled and got out of his car and into the squad car. "What about the old man?" Tracker asked.

"He's maggot meat," Bateman said, and pulled away from the roadside onto the deserted highway.

***

Aboriginal Elder William Parfitt woke to the sound of the car pulling up in the driveway. He sat up in the hammock on the veranda and watched as Bateman and Tracker got out of the car and walked over. There had to be something badly wrong for Tracker to be riding with a cop. He stood up and listened as they told him about Abe's unexpected death.

"Heart attack? But he was in good nick. Didn't eat

rubbish. Never touched a drop."

"He was under a lot of stress," Bateman said, "wouldn't sign the contract."

"Where is he now?"

"At the Creed County Morgue," Bateman said, offering William the clipboard. "Just sign off here," he said.

William looked at the contract, taking a moment to recognise what it was, and the implications. "What? What's this got to do—?"

"Just do it," Tracker said, "it's best for all of us now."

"I need to think about it," William said.

"Funny. That's just what Abe said," said Bateman, smirking. "Just before he carked it."

William looked up at Bateman, then at Tracker, who stood beside the officer. The message in their eyes was clear. William shuddered. Tracker had been a loose cannon for years and was known to dish out a hell of a beating to anybody, man or child, who angered him. But he had always respected Abe, never said a bad word about him. To think he had finally rebelled in the most shocking way imaginable was deeply disturbing, and William felt that the world he had known was suddenly turned on its head. He sat back in the hammock and Bateman put the pen in his hand. William signed the contract.

Chapter 16

The nurse kept the car door wide open as the cop leaned in and dragged Abe's corpse out of the squad car. He slung the body over his shoulder and carried it inside the Creed County Morgue, laying it gently down on the examination table as the coroner stood by, putting on his rubber gloves.

"Suspected heart attack," the cop said.

"Okay, thank you."

"No worries," the cop said and walked out. The nurse, already in her scrubs, stood by the body.

"Let's see if he had a heart attack," said the coroner, putting on a mask.

She leaned over Abe's face and carefully thumbed open one of his eyelids. The pupil constricted, startling her. Then the other eye opened, and she gasped, stepping back.

"Excuse me, miss," Abe said, hopping off the table.

The doctor watched, dumbfounded, as Abe walked out the front door.

***

Tracker led Ryan, Donna and Bateman through the bush, his eyes on the ground, searching for a broken twig, a rock that looked out of place or, even better, a footprint.

Bateman was lagging behind. His painkillers were wearing off, and he was struggling with the pain in his ankle. "I can't do this," he finally said.

"Fuck, you're soft," Ryan said.

"My foot's hanging from a bit of gristle. It's pissing blood and pus, you wanna smell?"

"That'll be the least of your worries if the kid gets away."

"I need medication."

"You just want a fix, junkie," Donna said. "Go on then, go! Nobody's got a gun to your head. Yet."

Bateman stopped and leant against a tree, raising his foot from the ground. "I'll be back," he said, then turned around and walked.

"Yeah, right," Donna said.

***

David ran deeper into the bush, leaping over logs and ducking overhanging branches, weaving through bushes and trees on his way back to the cave, as his grandfather had instructed. He didn't know what to make of his grandfather's actions. Had he really died? The old man had plenty of tricks, but David had never seen him fake dying. It sure didn't look like a trick.

He wondered about Tracker. He had seen Tracker take something from that bastard cop, and then abandon him and his grandfather. Why would Tracker betray them? As his mind and body raced, a rock under foot slid loose, and he tumbled over the scrub, the side of his face slamming hard into the trunk of a tree.

He reeled back in pain, tears rolling down his cheeks. *Granddad's dead,* he thought to himself. *He couldn't have faked that, he must'a died! Probably had a heart attack cos he saw Tracker betray us!* A wave of sadness overwhelmed him and he started sobbing.

"Get up!" he said to himself, and sprung to his feet. "No time for this, you gotta get moving!" With that, he set off running again.

***

Tom sat beneath a tree, eating some bush nuts with one hand, checking the phone with the other. Still no signal. It occurred to him to check the text messages. The first one he opened was from a "Sarge."

Show no mercy. Give them a flogging.

Then another:

No more Abos today. Full house! Good work!

Tom thought it was fair to assume that Sarge was Sgt. Watson, and was staggered that any police officer could be so vile and corrupt as to preside over what seemed to be organised brutality. But then, given the treatment he'd personally received, and knowing Watson had also been involved in the kidnapping of a young boy, he wasn't too surprised.

The envelope, bearing a police insignia, contained six stacks of hundred- dollar bills. He put it back in his pocket and noticed a very faint signal on the phone that quickly disappeared. He walked back and forth, holding the phone above his head, eyes on the screen.

He walked towards the riverbank, and it picked up a bar, then two, before dropping out. He walked closer still and the signal returned intermittently. He stood still on the bank, holding it high, when there was a sudden rush and splash of water. An enormous crocodile burst out of the river beside him, jaws wide open, a flash of white dagger teeth. Tom sprang sideways, the jaws snapping by his head, so close he could smell its putrid breath. The croc turned almost immediately and lunged again, but Tom was well clear now, sprinting through the reeds and into the thick bush.

***

"Will you stop going on about it?" Ryan said. "We'll find him, okay?" Donna shook her head, not convinced.

"We won't find anyone if youse keep yapping!" Tracker said, leading the way through the scrub.

"Exactly, so let's—"

"Shut up!" Tracker said, stopping still. Ryan and Donna stopped, and they could hear it too: someone crashing through the bush nearby. "It's a man," Tracker said, "coming this way."

Ryan pulled his gun and braced himself as the crashing grew louder, closer. Then the bushes next to them erupted, and a man, face covered in a tropical spider web, fell at their feet, hand-sized spiders crawling all over him. Donna knelt beside him and helped pull the web off his face, revealing Anthony.

"It's okay, they're not venomous," she said. "They won't hurt you."

He heaved and splattered, coughing up a mouthful of web.

"Give him some water," Ryan said, replacing his handgun. Donna unclipped a bottle from her belt and Anthony chugged down its contents.

"Are you hurt?" she asked.

He shook his head, panting. "Oh, thank Christ."

"What are you doing out here?"

"We were camping. Some maniac kidnapped a boy. We tried to help, he . . . he chased us, tried to kill us . . ." Tears streamed down his face.

"Were you camping with Tom McLaren?"

"Yeah. Yes! Is he okay?"

Donna took a notepad from her pocket and checked over some notes. "He's fine, love. You must be Anthony Rockeby, right?" He nodded, sitting up and wiping his eyes. "What about your other colleague, Edward Hitchens?" Donna asked.

"I had to leave him," he said, and started sobbing. She put an arm around him and he hugged her.

"He'll be okay love. We'll pick him up soon enough."

She unclipped her radio.

***

The pig dog was still on the scent, jerking the leash in Kris's hands, leading the skirmish line deep into the wilderness.

"Won't be long now," said Watson, sitting tall in the saddle. "He can taste it."

Donna's voice screeched through the radio on Watson's belt. "Bravo Whiskey to Papa, you there?"

He picked up the handpiece. "Go ahead, Bravo Whiskey."

"Request immediate assistance, meet at point alpha."

"I'm on my way," Watson said, then replaced the handpiece. "I'll catch up," he said to Kris. "He's a cop-killer. Don't forget it." She nodded, and he turned the horse around and set off at a gallop.

***

Anthony sat on the hood of a paddy wagon at the base of the cliff as Donna gently cleaned his face with a sterile wipe.

"Just close your eyes, love. That's it," she said.

Tracker stood in a cordoned-off area, examining the bloody rock that split Piper's skull. He heard something in the bush and quickly stepped away from the area, making himself scarce. Several minutes later, Watson appeared at the edge of the clearing on the horse. He dismounted, waved Donna over, and they talked privately.

"He doesn't know about Bateman, he just wants to go

home," she said. "He won't cause any problems, doesn't know anything."

"Has he seen Bateman?"

"Yeah, but he doesn't know he's a cop. I say we send him home. He'll never come back here, why would he? He's been traumatised. Victims of trauma don't return to the scene of trauma, you know that!"

Sgt. Watson nodded and smiled at her. "Let's go and have a chat with him," he said.

They approached Anthony. "This is my dad, Sgt. Watson," Donna said.

"You've had a pretty rough time of it, mate," Watson said.

"You have no idea."

"Well, don't worry about it. You'll be home in no time."

"Thank you, I can't tell you how much I would love to be at home right now."

"We'll get you to the airport right away. I'll take you myself."

"Thanks so much."

"No worries, least I can do. But I'm afraid I'll have to ask you to ride in the back of the wagon, if you don't mind?"

Donna opened her mouth to speak, then turned away.

Anthony looked at the back of the paddy wagon, a dark chamber with two small windows on the rear doors, designed to house prisoners for transportation.

"This the right one?" Watson asked Ryan, pointing to

the paddy wagon. Ryan nodded. "We have certain protocols for transportation. You're a lawyer, right? You understand."

Anthony nodded. He didn't care how he travelled; he just wanted to get going.

Watson opened the rear doors and helped Anthony climb inside. He shut the doors and nodded to Ryan, who locked them with a key.

"Leave him inside till he's stone cold," Watson said.

Donna's eyes were watering as she lit up a cigarette.

"I thought you quit!" Sgt. Watson said.

"Don't, Dad," she said, with a tone of rebuke he recognised.

"I'll be on the radio if you need me," Watson said and walked towards his horse.

Anthony sat inside the paddy wagon, watching through the mesh glass windows as Watson mounted his horse. Maybe they decided someone else should drive, he thought. He looked over to Donna, who was smoking. The other cop sat down on a log, also showing Anthony his back.

"Come on, people."

Tracker walked over to Donna and after they spoke, he stared at Anthony as if in curiosity. Anthony found it disturbing and slid further back into the darkened chamber, when he heard something stirring behind him. He turned to see a large, black snake with a copper-toned head that was elevated and poised to strike.

"Jesus!" he said, scrambling over to the door. The snake

shot its tongue in and out repeatedly, its head swaying slowly, assessing Anthony. He turned to the window. "There's a snake in here! Hey! Help! Let me out!"

Tracker kept still, watching him like a child fascinated by a fly in a spider's web.

"Help! Please!"

Anthony's scream made Donna shudder. She put her headphones on, cranked up the volume of the music on her phone and closed her eyes.

Chapter 17

Tom knew he was safe from the crocodile but kept running anyway. He ran till he came out of the bush to a vast, open expanse of rock, with scattered boulders. This place was unlike anything he'd seen before, otherworldly. There were flat sheets of rock layered upon each other like piles of massive roof tiles that had been dumped haphazardly; bright yellow rocks striped with rust brown lines in a distinct zebra skin pattern; dark rocks with flashes of silver, red and purple that made them look like they were on fire. The place was at once beautiful and eerie. Perhaps he could get a signal from the top of one of those mounds, he thought.

The boulders were large and difficult to climb, but he crawled up to the top of a pile and took out the mobile phone. There was one bar of signal. Squinting in the searing sun, he dialled Claire's number.

***

Hundreds of kilometres away at a pearl farm, Claire was in campaign mode. With a media circus filming her every step, she walked along with a pearl farmer, who told her the ins and outs of the business. Claire nodded and smiled, and asked perceptive questions as Drake kept an eye on the proceedings. The mobile phone in Drake's pocket rang, and she took it out. She didn't recognise the number and so rejected the call, switched the phone off and put it back in her pocket.

***

Tom thought about calling triple zero, but dismissed the idea. The call would most likely get diverted to the local police. He had plenty of friends and colleagues he could call back in Perth, but he didn't remember phone numbers. He was surprised he had remembered Claire's. Still pondering, he put his hand in his pocket and felt something inside. It was a business card, covered in mud. He wiped it clean, seeing the name Hannah Simpson, and remembered it was the young journalist whom he had met after the meeting with the Elders. Could he trust her? He couldn't be sure, but at the very least, he could get her confidentiality by promising her a big, exclusive story, which he would deliver. Just not the story she was expecting. He dialled the number.

***

The Toyota rental drove along the main street in Creed, Hannah at the wheel. The phone in her bag rang, and she pulled it out and answered.

"Hello, is that Hannah?" Tom asked.

"Speaking."

"This is Tom McLaren."

"Sorry, I can't hear you."

"Tom McLaren here."

"Who is this?" she said, pushing the phone closer to her ear. Then she saw the motorcycle cop riding beside her, signalling for her to pull over. "Fuck." She pulled onto the shoulder of the road, wondering how much she was going to have to cough up for speaking on her phone while driving.

***

The phone went dead and Tom looked at the screen. One bar was not going to be enough from out here. Where to now? He looked over the rocks back to the bush and noticed it was thicker as it followed the contours of the river. Perhaps there would be another town along the river. He started making his way back down.

Chapter 18

Tom walked through the bush following the course of the river, grateful for the shade. He stopped and took a sip from the dead cop's water bottle, careful to ration himself to only a couple of mouthfuls. As he replaced the cap, he heard a dog barking. He turned in a slight panic. Had to be a police dog, he thought. It wasn't far behind. There was no way he could outrun a dog. Perhaps he could hide his scent in the stream and cross over to the other side, further downstream. But the stream would slow him down, allow them to get closer. They may have been on both sides of the river anyway.

What's the point? How do I evade a dog? The dog will most likely be on a leash, which means I only have to outrun the cop holding the leash.

He turned and launched into a run.

***

The dog led Kris ahead of the skirmish line of cops, the animal growling and whining in excitement.

"What's your hurry?" yelled Senior Constable Marsh, red faced and dripping sweat.

"We're close now," Kris called back. Her concern was that the alleged cop-killer had already heard the dog and would be prepared for them. She wanted to minimise his reaction time. The leash was taut, the dog jerking her forward in a frenzy of excitement.

Marsh and the others, all in their thirties, forties and fifties and nowhere near as fit as Kris, watched as she broke away, disappearing over a small ridge. Marsh stopped, buckling over to catch his breath. "We're not Olympic runners, for fuck sake."

***

The river became a waterfall, and Tom stood on the bank looking over a sheer cliff, about a five-storey drop. The gorge was about ten car lengths across, another sheer cliff on the other side. Tom spotted a rickety wooden pedestrian bridge to his left, a short run from where he stood.

***

Kris was running at full tilt with the dog leash in one hand, her Glock in the other. They burst through the scrub and over logs and shrubs, the dog growling and whining with excitement. It leapt over a thigh-high rock, and Kris jumped after it, but her knee smashed against the blunt rock on the way down. She dropped the leash and tumbled to the ground, clutching her knee. The dog bolted ahead and vanished in the bush.

***

He came to the footbridge, a twisted old wooden construction that hadn't been used in years, maybe decades. There was a gap where the first few floor planks should have been, a perilous drop below. The rest of the decking didn't look safe, chequered with planks that were missing or broken. The handrail on the right side was missing completely.

"They'd be insane to follow me," he said out loud, taking hold of the left handrail. He stepped onto the beam beneath it, and sidestepped his way out past the gap. He eased a foot onto some floor planks, and they creaked and bent under his weight. *Stick to the railing.* He continued sidestepping his way out along the bridge, the railing swaying and groaning. He looked down at the treacherous drop to the rocky stream below. There would be no surviving a fall from here.

As he got further along, he could see a gap in the handrail up ahead. He heard the dog barking behind him and turned to see the animal inspecting the gap at the bridgehead. Clearly, the animal didn't like the look of it, and stayed put on solid ground, pacing left and right. Tom recognised it was the same dog that he had trapped in the tent and clobbered with the gas bottle. *Should have hit it a few more times, finished it off,* he thought.

He hustled, ignoring the sway of the handrail, sidestepping faster as the dog barked at him. He soon came to the end of the handrail and glanced back to see the dog bounding over the gap and landing safely on the planks.

Tom stepped cautiously onto the floor planking, and it bent beneath him. He crouched, then lay down and spread himself over several of the planks, dispersing his weight, and started crawling. The other side of the gorge was still a world away.

He pushed on, passing several planks, then looked over his shoulder and saw the dog skilfully choosing its paw placement and steadily advancing towards him. With its weight spread over four legs, it was able to tread where Tom could not and so could move faster. It was clear the animal was going to reach him soon enough.

He sat up and noticed the loose section of dangling handrail, and thought it might make a useful weapon. He crawled back to the railing and grabbed a hold of it. The rusty iron bolt that held it in place would not give. The snarling dog was almost upon him, threatening, warning him to quit. He yanked at the loose section, and the dog snapped, sinking its teeth into his shoe; not to do any damage, but to demonstrate its power. He released the stubborn rail and the dog released his foot. He turned and faced the animal as it straddled his legs, snarling, baring its fangs. *When it gets close enough, grab its collar and try to keep it from biting, then ram your knees into its chest and shove it right over the edge.* The dog stepped closer, muscles rippling, saliva dripping from its open mouth. Trying to outwrestle this beast was going to be a tall order.

But he didn't get the chance. The plank beneath Tom's

thighs gave way, and both he and the animal dropped. Tom's hands sprung out, and he grabbed a hold of the beam beneath the handrail, legs dangling. He pulled his torso up onto the beam and looked down to see the dead animal lying on the rocks below, its intestines sprayed out of its ruptured torso. Tom looked at the bridge before him. There were huge gaps, and the absence of handrails meant he would have to crawl along the side beam for more than half the length, during which time the police could arrive and shoot him. He decided to head back. With no dog to track him, he figured the odds of escaping had improved.

He was almost at the end of the bridge when he saw the cop standing in the trees with her gun drawn on him.

"Keep coming," Kris said.

"Why? So you can shoot me?"

"I don't want to shoot you, but there are a dozen cops headed this way, and they do. They think you're a cop-killer."

"And what do you think?"

"I think that's a decision for a court of law. I want to take you in alive to make sure you get there." The voices of the approaching cops grew louder. "But I can't guarantee your protection when they get here."

He jumped the gap in the decking and stepped onto solid ground. She kept the gun on him.

"Now get on the ground, face down," she said.

"We don't have time," he said, the voices getting nearer.

***

Senior Constable Marsh led the men through the bush.

"Looks like he's headed for the old bridge," one of the men said, looking at a map on his phone.

"I sure as Shazza's shit ain't crossing that old bridge!" Marsh said. They stepped into a clearing where Kris was sitting on the ground, the leg of her pants rolled up, exposing her bloody, grazed knee.

"You lost the dog! I told you to slow down!"

"You got any Betadine?"

"Anybody?" Marsh asked. Someone came forward and handed Kris a small bottle of disinfectant. She dabbed a little on the wound.

"So which way?" Marsh asked.

"He went south, I think."

"That's a relief," said Marsh, grateful the dog hadn't headed for the bridge.

"The dog's probably got the cop-killer pinned to the ground, waiting for you guys," she said.

"You gonna be all right?"

"Yeah, I'll catch up," Kris said.

"You'll know when we find him. Just follow the gunshots," Marsh said. With that, the cops moved on.

Kris pulled the leg of her pants down and walked over to a large, hollowed-out tree. "All clear," she said. Tom stepped out, feeling reasonably confident he could trust her now. "Now put these on," she said, holding out a pair of handcuffs.

"You think that's wise, with your trigger-happy friends around?"

"Put them on, or I'll put them on for you."

He took the handcuffs and hurled them into the gorge. She charged him, pushing him into the hollow trunk against the inner wall, put a hand on his mouth and signalled for him to be quiet. She turned around, took her phone, switched on the camera, and stuck the lens just out of the hollow. On the screen, they saw Sgt. Watson approaching on horseback. He hadn't seen them. She switched the camera off and pocketed the phone, pushing firmly against Tom.

The clip-clopping of the horse drew nearer and then passed them, so close they could have leaned out and touched it. The horse whinnied.

"Easy, we're not crossing the bridge," Watson said, and kept going.

They stayed absolutely still as the clip-clopping moved away. Then it stopped, and Tom wondered if the cop could see their footprints. Kris started adjusting something, and then suddenly she had loosened her pants and slid them down to her ankles. Baffled by her actions, Tom remained perfectly still as heavy boots landed on the ground, crunching the dry leaves beneath them. Then he saw the end of a rifle just outside.

"Hey!" Kris yelled. "I'm taking a shit in here!"

"Christ, I almost took your head off!"

"What do you want me to do? Crouch down in front of all the guys?"

"No, of course not. Sorry."

Tom could hear the guy stepping away and mounting the horse.

“They’re headed south along the ridge,” she said. “Can’t be more than a few minutes away.”

“Do you need anything? Paper?”

“Please leave,” she said firmly.

“Right. Wait, where’s my dog?”

“With the guys.”

“Goodo,” he said, then rode away.

Kris stood up, pulling on her pants, then buckling up her belt.

***

They came to the clearing at the base of the cliff, and Tom stayed well hidden in the bush as Kris surveyed the area for any other cops. She finally called him over and led him to the paddy wagon, taking the keys from the ignition.

“Under the circumstances, you won’t mind riding in the back,” she said, walking around to the rear doors.

“Probably safer that way,” he said.

She unlocked the door, and it swung open, Anthony’s head and shoulders falling out of the vehicle. He was a repulsive sight, his face bloated and contorted, dry foam around his mouth. Tom stared in shock. “Anthony,” he said. Then he put a finger to Anthony’s throat and felt for a pulse. But he was stone cold and there wasn’t one.

The torso of the snake slid around Anthony, startling Tom, and he stepped back. Kris shoved Anthony back in and shut the door.

“Taipan,” she said, “horrible way to go. I’m so sorry.”

Tom stood motionless, his expression blank. “We have

to find another vehicle with keys in it," she said. But he didn't hear her and turned away, sitting on the ground, a lump building in his throat. She returned soon after and saw that he was still in a state of shock.

"Okay, let's roll," she said. He didn't appear to hear her. "I'm very sorry about your friend. Truly. But we have to move."

He nodded and followed her to another car.

***

The hunting party was gathered on the cliff, looking out over the perilous bridge. Watson stood beside his horse, his binoculars set on the remains of his dog on the rocks below. He felt a sting of pain in his chest. There was no sign of the lawyer's body.

"I guess the cop-killer made it across," Marsh said.

"I guess," agreed Watson.

"You don't expect us to cross, do ya?" said Marsh.

Watson put down the binoculars and looked at Marsh. "There's another way round, set us back an hour or so. Put somebody here in case he backtracks."

Marsh nodded.

"Any news from Derby Police?" Watson asked.

"They're delivering their dogs by chopper. Shouldn't be more than an hour," Marsh said.

"Goodo."

***

The police sedan cruised along the outback highway, Kris

at the wheel. Tom lay on the back seat silently weeping, his face screwed up, hands clenched into fists.

"Can you describe the man?"

He gathered himself. "Mid-thirties. Blonde hair. Caucasian. Chafed arms. I think he's a vegetarian."

"Raspy voice?"

"Yeah."

"That's Bateman for sure. What the hell are they up to?"

Tom pulled the mobile phone from his pocket and flicked to the messages page. He sat up and handed it to her as a police car raced by in the opposite direction. "This belonged to the dead cop," he said, ducking back down.

"Stay down, or you'll end up like your friend back there."

"Right. Keep an eye out for a grey-haired guy on foot, will you?"

"Your other colleague?"

"My friend. Ed's not in great shape."

"Sure thing. Damn, I knew there was something going on when I caught Sarge destroying the DVR. But kidnapping?" she said, shaking her head in a mix of disbelief and disgust. "Why the hell would Sarge get involved in that?"

"What are the most common motives for kidnapping?"

"Mostly, it's related to child custody. Then there's the sickos, perverts."

"Does the sergeant strike you as a sicko or a pervert?"

"Absolutely not. In fact, he doesn't take too kindly to those types."

Tom took the envelope from his pocket and spilled the money out onto the front seat. "That was also in the cop's jacket," he said. She noticed the police insignia on the envelope.

"Boy, oh boy!"

"Why would they spend so much? What makes the boy so valuable?"

"His family don't have any money. No assets to speak of."

"You sure about that?"

She thought for a moment. "The land?"

"Their community is sitting on the largest uranium deposit on the planet. Expensive real estate. If the deal goes through, they're looking at a huge payout. The cops might want some of that action. The kid's grandfather won't give it up, maybe they wanted to change his mind."

"That land's gotta be worth billions, right?"

"To QPEC Mining, yeah. A fraction of that for the current custodians. But a fraction of a billion goes an awfully long way."

They took a bend in the road, and Kris saw a police roadblock up ahead, two cops standing by their squad cars. "Oh, shit." She hit a button on the dash, and the siren wailed, blue lights flashing over the bonnet. She pulled a hard, one-hundred-and-eighty-degree turn, Tom sliding against the door. The two cops didn't give her a second look.

"Problem?" Tom said.

"They've already locked down the roads," Kris said.

"We'll have to think of something else."

Chapter 19

David stood perfectly still on the bank of the river, knees bent, eyes fixed on something in the dark, slow-flowing water. It looked like a couple of knobs on a submerged branch. But David knew better.

"I see you, big fella," he whispered. He looked over to a large rock in the river, just a few feet out from the bank. Above the rock, a sturdy branch, extending from a tree on the bank. He considered the distance from the rock to the branch—a fair leap—then looked over to the muddy bank, where he could see crocodile tracks. He looked back at the croc, catching a glimpse of one of its eyelids opening, the eye looking straight at him. *You could get me right now, if you wanted, big fella. But you're a bit lazy. Maybe you got a bellyful already? Maybe you want me to come closer so you don't have to run?*

"You be nice now, big fella," he said. Then he took a long, deep breath, and ran for the rock in the river.

***

Tracker knew he was close when he arrived at the riverbank and caught sight of David's tracks in the mud, along with the fresh croc tracks, which indicated that the reptile had lunged out of the water at a deadly speed.

"Croc tracks?" Donna asked.

"Yeah, big one," Tracker said.

"Are those the boy's tracks?"

Tracker nodded.

"Well, I think we can call off the search," Ryan said.

"It's about bloody time we had a bit of luck. Natural causes, too!" Donna said, as Tracker kept studying the mess of tracks in the mud. Donna picked up her radio. "This is Bravo Whiskey, you there, Papa?"

"Right here, Bravo Whiskey," came Sgt. Watson's voice.

"Looks like the rabbit got taken by a croc."

"I didn't say that," Tracker said.

"Stand by for confirmation," Donna said.

Tracker pointed to the rock sticking out of the water. Donna and Ryan didn't understand what Tracker was getting at. They didn't see the muddy mark on the top of the rock the same way he did. They couldn't see that the smudge was left by a child's foot. Tracker pointed up to the overhanging branch, followed it along to the trunk where it had been broken slightly on the upper side. Broken from strain, from bearing weight. A child's weight. Tracker pictured the boy running to the rock, leaping up to the branch as the croc leapt out of the water. He imagined the boy scurrying over to the far side of the trunk, and then confirmed what he imagined—the bark around the tree was damaged, showed signs of something sliding across the surface.

With great caution, Tracker walked closer to the river, to the trunk of the tree, keeping an eye on the river. He searched the reeds, and soon found some that were slightly bent. They had been pushed to the ground and had sprung back up. He searched the mud at the base of the reeds and found what he was looking for: half a child's footprint. The boy had run on his toes, fleeing for his life. There were more croc prints nearby, but Tracker followed the boy's and could see David had escaped.

"Clever boy," he said. "He fooled you lot!"

"So the croc didn't get him?" Donna said, stepping closer to the riverbank.

Tracker shook his head.

"Scratch that, Papa," she said into the radio. "Disregard previous message."

"Copy that," Watson said. "Hey, Bravo Whiskey, you seen or heard anything from Kris?"

"Negative."

"Careful," Tracker said. "Old mate's in there."

She shuffled away from the bank.

***

David skirted along the edge of the rusty red gorge like a bird skipping along a wire, only he didn't have wings to save him; one misstep and he would hurtle down the jagged drop to rocky rapids below. That morning, he and

Tom had walked the same path, only in the opposite direction, and come from the same place he was heading to now—the Dreaming Cave. He had been told never to take an outsider there, but he had no choice. Besides, Tom wouldn't tell anyone about it, he was sure. He was a good bloke.

He looked back over his shoulder, then dropped to a crouch, seeing the three distant figures emerging from the bush and walking to the edge of the gorge. He immediately froze upon recognising one of them. There was no mistaking that figure—the chest so broad his arms were forced to swing out away from his body as he walked; the bulging forearms; the mop of hair. It was Tracker, no question about it.

David stopped breathing, his pulse thumping in his throat. The other two were cops. At this distance, he couldn't make out their faces, but that didn't matter. There was no hiding his trail from Tracker. Even over hard rock, Tracker could see tells. David's mind raced. He might not be able to hide his tracks, but he could go a lot faster than Tracker and the cops, and he could climb up and down rocks and through narrow paths and spaces that would be very difficult for Tracker to follow, maybe impossible.

David had convinced himself that Abe's death was an act, a planned distraction intended to buy David time to escape. Abe had told him to go to the Dreaming Cave, and he must have intended to meet him there, to help him. Abe was the only person David knew who could stand up to Tracker.

He started breathing again, still anxious but also confident that he had more than a good chance. He crawled to the edge of the gorge and stuck his head straight out over the drop. Scanning the rock wall, he soon found what he was looking for, about a third of the way down: a deep groove cut into the side of the cliff wall, a natural path. The overhanging rock meant he would be hidden from Tracker and the cops if they stayed on the top of the gorge. They would have to follow him down and along a dangerous passage or risk losing him.

He spotted a rock jutting out a few feet below. Hanging onto a slit on the edge, David carefully eased himself over, toes sliding down the rough rock, burning from friction as gravity pulled him down the face of the steep wall. Toes and arms stretched to their limits, he still couldn't feel the rock he was hoping to use as a foothold. Certain that he was above it, he let go and dropped. A deep pang of fear and nausea rose in his gut as he thought he had misjudged the drop. Then he stopped abruptly, the balls of his feet landing on the rock. He could see the path just a few feet below to his left. There were plenty of fissures and niches in the wall, which he grabbed, making his way over to the deep groove. He climbed into the groove, which was like a very narrow half tunnel, cut naturally into the wall. It was only wide enough for him to put one foot in front of the other, but it kept him out of sight from anyone above. To his right was the deadly drop. The tunnel wall provided plenty of cracks and jutting rocks for handholds. Keeping his eyes in front, he shuffled forward, soon gathering confidence and moving fairly quickly.

Chapter 20

Kris drove along the suburban street, watching the car that had just passed in her rearview mirror until it turned a corner and disappeared. The street was empty, but that didn't mean there weren't eyes on her. Some of the neighbours, especially the retired elderly couple opposite her place, were almost as good as CCTV surveillance and never missed a chance to report unusual happenings to her. Tom lay low on the seat as she pulled into her drive, going all the way to the front door. She got out and had one last look before ushering him inside.

A little later, he was seated in the dining room with a towel around his waist, having showered. Kris came in carrying a first aid kit and sat beside him.

"I've washed your clothes, or what was left of them. They're in the dryer, shouldn't be long."

"Thanks," he said.

She took a cotton bud, dipped it in disinfectant and dabbed a cut on his shoulder. The sting made him wince.

"There's a bloke I know, pilot. Owns a Cessna. He can

fly us to Darwin at first light. That's our best bet."

"You trust him?"

"Absolutely. He's like family," she said, taking a pair of tweezers from the first aid kit. "This might sting a bit," she said, taking hold of a nasty little thorn lodged in his back. She pulled it out, and a pinhead of blood replaced it, which she dabbed.

"You've sure got a good sample of the local plant life here. I think you got at least one of every known species. Might even have some new ones."

Tom didn't respond, his thoughts having returned to Anthony. She noticed his torso was rigid with tension.

"You're safe here, you know. You can relax a little bit."

He nodded.

She placed a hand on his neck and he flinched slightly. Then he realised what she was doing and closed his eyes, enjoying her soothing hands as she gently massaged him. As he sank into the chair, he began to feel the sting and ache of the dozens of cuts and bruises that he somehow hadn't noticed before. This was followed by a cocktail of emotion swelling deep in his chest and stomach—loss, grief, anger and panic.

He stood up, startling her. "Thanks, but I'll relax when we land in Darwin."

"Oh, okay then," she said, thinking she must have crossed the line. "Yeah, I better get back to work."

"It's not that I don't appreciate it, I just . . ."

"No worries. I should go, anyway. Could be some incriminating evidence in the station. Now everybody's out looking for you, it's probably a good time to go check."

"Dead lawyer in the back of a police van not enough?"

"No," she said, "it's not. They might have found him dead for all we know. They could spin it any way they want. You're looking at a murder charge, witnessed by a police officer. You're going to need some solid evidence." She walked to the door. "I'm arming the alarm, so don't open the doors or windows. And just so you know, most of the local cops live in this neighbourhood."

"I feel safer already. Hey, um, thanks. I appreciate it."

She gave him a half smile, nodded, and then she was gone.

Chapter 21

Looking over the rocky gorge, Tracker groaned. "Little bastard's gone over the edge."

"You mean he fell?" Donna asked, a glint of hope in her voice.

"Nah, he's climbed down because he thinks we won't follow him."

"He's right about that," said Ryan.

"What do you think, we should just pack up and go home?" Donna said.

"I never said that," Ryan said.

"So what are you saying?"

"I'm saying I'm not going down there, and I'm pretty sure you're not going either," Ryan said.

"Wrong," she said. "What about you?" she asked Tracker. "Can you get down there?"

"No need," Tracker said. "I know where he's going. Further up river, there's a cave on top of the gorge. Good hiding place. That's where he's heading."

"Can we get there walking along the top?" Donna

asked.

“Yeah, but we need someone to follow him, in case he backtracks.”

“No sense asking you, is there?” Donna asked Ryan.

Tracker sniggered, “You got bigger balls than he does.”

“You’re not really going down there, are ya?” Ryan asked.

“Out of the way,” she said, and stepped by him.

Tracker pointed her in the direction of the deep groove that cut along the rock wall, which he was certain David had taken. He and Ryan watched as she lowered herself over the side of the cliff and dropped to the ledge, then made her way over to the half tunnel, giving them the thumbs up before entering. Tracker and Ryan headed along the edge of the cliff top.

***

When David finally emerged from a dark alcove at the top of the cliff, he was exhausted, his throat burning and his fingertips and feet raw from the rough rocks he had climbed over. He headed up to the cave mouth he and Tom had emerged from that morning.

Chapter 22

Tom still had the towel around his waist as he crouched down in front of the dryer. He had leaned right in and grabbed his clothes when he noticed the biggest spider he had ever seen, perched on the dryer controls in front of his face. He jumped backwards instinctively. Looking around the room, he found a cricket bat that would do nicely. He held the bat over the creature and gave it a nudge, watching it scurry down the side of the machine. He took his clothes from the dryer.

Dressed in his tattered clothes, he sauntered through the lounge, passing framed photos of Kris with what appeared to be friends and family, and in her police uniform at a primary school, surrounded by smiling Aboriginal children.

A little later, he was dressed and sitting in front of a desktop computer in the lounge room. He wondered if she would mind him using it, but figured since she had left the username and password written on a Post-it note, she probably wouldn't, and probably didn't use it very often herself. He went online and searched for "Dawn Konnigan QPEC" and turned up dozens of links to news stories. One story caught his attention. He opened the link and read the article:

> Q-PEC CEO DAWN KONNIGAN CLEARED OF EXTORTION CHARGES
> *QPEC CEO Dawn Konnigan was cleared of all charges, including assault and extortion . . .*
>
> *. . . Konnigan has a history of employing violent criminals . . .*

The article included a picture of Konnigan with her driver standing beside her, named in the article as Lewis Rooke. Tom conducted a new search on Rooke and found some alarming results:

> FEDERAL POLICE OFFICER LINKED TO ORGANISED CRIME RACKETS
> *Officer Lewis Rooke, a parliamentary bodyguard, has been linked to known underworld figures . . .*
>
> *. . . lack of evidence, Rooke was dismissed from duty, no charges laid . . .*
>
> *Rooke, a prime suspect in assassination of businessman . . . links to other businessmen who have died in suspicious circumstances . . .*

Chapter 23

It was evening when Kris arrived at the police station, and as she stepped out of her car, she questioned her own judgement. *How could you leave a suspect unattended in your house? What if he really is a cop-killer?* She quickly dismissed the thought. He was a big-city lawyer. What motive would he have for killing a Kimberley cop? None had been given by Donna Watson, who reported Piper's death. No explanation had been provided about why Watson and Piper were standing on the edge of a dangerous cliff. Then there was Sgt. Watson's destruction of the digital video recorder. It was clear to Kris that her colleagues were involved in criminal activity.

She walked through the front door and soon found that the station was completely unattended. It was eerie, not to mention in breach of protocol. She could only assume Watson was in a state of panic that led him to send every cop he had on the search. She remembered how he had made it clear to all, in no uncertain terms, that Tom was a cop-killer, knowing that would trigger an emotional response from them. He had given the distinct impression that he would look after anyone who shot Tom on sight. Then she caught herself making assumptions and backed up. *Stay objective. You don't have all the facts.*

She stopped outside Sgt. Watson's office and stood perfectly still, listening. There was still no sign or sound of anyone, so she went in and rifled through the paperwork on the desk, seeing nothing out of the ordinary. She went through his drawers, shelves, notebook and diary. Still nothing. Sitting in his reclining chair, she looked over everything he would look over, then noticed the rubbish bin in the corner, full of scrunched-up notes, chocolate wrappers and other junk. She pulled the garbage bag out of the bin and tied it up.

"You on cleaning duties?" the young cop said, standing outside Watson's office, startling her. "You can clean my desk when you're done," he said with a smile.

"Piss off!" Kris said, her heart in her mouth. The guy sniggered and went about his business. Kris took the bag and left.

Chapter 24

The police car was parked in the dimly lit street outside Kris's house, the engine still running. Watching the silhouetted figure inside the lounge, sitting at the computer by the window, the driver scratched his chafed forearm.

Inside the house, Tom thought it was likely, however disturbing and disappointing, that Konnigan was behind David's abduction for the purpose of blackmailing the Elders, and that Rooke was most likely involved, probably as a middleman. Tom turned away from the computer and leaned back in his chair, gazing over to the window. He froze in astonishment. Between the curtains, he could see Bateman's face, looking straight at him. He blinked and the face was gone. Had he hallucinated? His instincts said *no*, and he leapt out of the chair a split second before the window shattered from an incoming terra-cotta pot.

The house alarm screamed as Tom scrambled out of the room, switching off the light on his way in the hope that the darkness would buy him some time, even if just a few seconds.

It worked. Bateman dropped through the window

frame with a flashlight on, pistol drawn, scanning the room. He heard the back door open, then the fly screen slam shut. He bolted through the lounge and found his way to the open back door. Standing in the doorway, he shone the light out into the backyard, scanning left and right. Bateman turned instinctively to check his back, but he was too late to avoid the swinging cricket bat, the *whack*! knocking him out cold.

Kris was almost home when she heard her alarm blaring. As she approached, she noticed the police car parked outside. She wondered if Tom had tried to flee. Moments later, she stalked into the bathroom, gun drawn, and found Tom gagging Bateman with duct tape as he lay unconscious, hands cuffed around the steel plumbing beneath the sink.

"Oh boy," Kris said, lowering her gun.

"Watto to Bateman, come in," called Sgt. Watson over Bateman's radio. "Come in, Bates, it's Watto here."

"I take it this is Bateman?" Tom asked.

"You seen him before?"

"You know I have."

"Where?"

"He's the guy who kidnapped the boy, chased us through the bush, et cetera. But you knew that."

"Yeah, I did. Just wanted you to confirm without me leading you—"

"I get it."

Kris reached down and took the radio from Bateman's belt. She then located his mobile phone and took that as well.

“Let’s go,” she said.

Bateman’s eyes flickered open, and he caught a glimpse of Kris and Tom walking towards the front door.

Chapter 25

Kris pulled over in a dark, empty street, stopping on the roadside. Tom sat beside her.

"So when do we meet your friend with the plane?"

"We'll meet him at an airstrip at dawn. In the meantime, we'll just have to hang low, find some place safe for you to sleep."

"I'm not concerned about sleep," Tom said. "How did Bateman know where to find me?"

"I don't know. I guess seeing as I'm the only cop not out looking for you, they wanted to know what I was up to. He couldn't have known you were there, that was just unfortunate."

"I imagine it's probably dangerous for you now."

"Seeing as they want your secrets to die with you, I would say so, yeah." She reached over to the back seat and grabbed the plastic bag full of Sgt. Watson's rubbish. "I got this from Watson's office. I'm going to go through it. Keep your eyes open, you might see something I miss; something important."

"Sure," he said, and watched as she put on a pair of

surgical gloves, then proceeded to empty the contents, piece by piece, into another plastic bag. She dug through snotty tissues, orange peel and screwed-up paper and soon pulled out a scrunched-up note. She showed him, and after a shake of his head, she dumped it into the second bag. She took another note.

"This could be something," she said, opening it so he could read it.

—WATSON: $35,000
—BATEMAN: $10,000
—GREY: $10,000
—PIPER: $10,000
—JACKSON: $5,000
Total: $70,000

"It's a pay sheet," she said. "Who gets what. They're all cops, except Jackson."

"Seventy grand," he said.

"This is solid."

"Shame it doesn't say who's handing out the cash," Tom said.

"Doesn't matter, I'd like to see Watson explain this to a jury," said Kris.

"It doesn't prove anything. Could be the tally from a game of Monopoly."

She put it in a snap-lock bag and sealed it. "It's a good start."

He nodded, and she pulled out a torn appointment

note, words and letters missing.

"Weds. Nicholls Room. L. Rooke," she read.

"L. Rooke. Lewis Rooke. That's Konnigan's driver."

"Why would Watson meet with the driver?" Kris asked.

"Konnigan's not going to meet these people directly. That's Rooke's department."

She sealed that note as well. They searched through the rest of the rubbish, finding nothing of apparent importance. Then she looked at the bag with the torn note. "The Nicholls Room . . ." her mind searching. "It's a conference room. At the Baudin Hotel," she said. She started the engine.

Chapter 26

David sat by a small fire on a natural mezzanine floor that curved all around the wall, overlooking the cave mouth. He was tired and hungry, and filled with an overwhelming sense of dread. Tracker could probably guess where David had gone. He would show up before too long. What could David do? Tracker knew this place better than he did. His thoughts were interrupted by a loud guttural sound nearby, like a large reptile, approaching from the shadows. David took a burning stick from the fire and retreated as the noise became louder, deeper, more threatening. He backed up beside the fire. It was too late to run now. Then he adopted a kind of combat pose, wide-eyed and focused. He swung the flaming stick like a warrior, projecting great ferocity and strength, concealing the terror that brimmed inside him.

The reptilian noise intensified and he turned directly towards it. A figure emerged, the horrible sound much louder now. He braced himself for combat as the figure stepped into the light. It was his grandfather, Abe, making the sound with a small woodwind instrument. He smiled at

David, and they embraced, tears of relief and joy filling David's eyes.

A little later, they sat by the fire, Abe sharpening the blade of a nulla-nulla, a wooden weapon that resembled an axe. David was sharpening a spear.

"No more kids' stuff, getting into trouble. Time for you to be a man now, be responsible."

David nodded his head solemnly. "Why did Dad sell us out to the cops?"

"He's lost his way, that one. Don't worry. I'll deal with him."

"What are you gonna do?"

"He'll be outcast, never come back."

"But maybe he didn't mean it, didn't know what he was doing."

"He's no good. Forget about him."

"I can't just forget about my dad."

"Tracker's not your father."

"What are you talking about?"

"He should have told you this himself. Years ago, when Tracker was in lockup, a couple of blackfellas from down the coast came around." Abe continued with the story, and by the end of it, David was speechless.

"You're still my grandson. You're part of our mob. We been here for thousands of years, living off this land. You'll live off it too." Abe tossed the nulla-nulla over to David and he caught it. "And protect it," Abe said.

Chapter 27

The night market was bustling with tourists, none of whom paid much attention to the police car parked on the kerb, or the passenger in the front seat. Tom kept his eyes down and was wishing Kris would hurry the hell up when his door swung open. Kris tossed a handful of clothes at him: a Hawaiian shirt, a shirt with koalas, a straw fedora, a baseball cap, and a pair of board shorts.

"Take your pick," she said.

She climbed in and drove away from the kerb as Tom got changed, choosing the Hawaiian shirt and the fedora. Soon she was parked on another busy roadside outside the Baudin Hotel. Cafes, bars and restaurants lined the street, streams of people going in and out, enjoying the warm night and the buzzing atmosphere. Kris and Tom walked into the hotel and approached the clerk behind the desk. Kris asked him if he was aware of any meetings in the Nicholls Room the previous Wednesday. The clerk had no memory of any specific meeting. He handed them a logbook and stated that the Nicholls Room was their most popular conference room. Kris and Tom looked over the previous Wednesday and found several bookings under various names, but none under the names of Rooke or Watson.

"Do you have CCTV footage inside the room?" Kris asked.

"Not inside it, but we do have it in the lobby, which any guest would obviously walk through to get to the Nicholls Room."

A moment later, the clerk was playing the footage through the computer mounted on the desk.

***

His hands cuffed around the plumbing under the sink, Bateman pulled himself up, putting his face close to his fingertips. He picked at the corner of the tape and peeled it off his mouth, sucking in air like he'd been holding his breath. He squirmed, trying to reach his belt. Contorted, arching his back, he groaned in pain as he raised his midsection. Finally, his fingertips touched a pouch on his belt. He tried to flick it open, wheezing, sweat pouring down his face. But his shoes slipped on the tiles, his buttocks slamming to the laundry floor. He tried again, and this time, he was able to hold himself just long enough to flick the pouch open and pull out his second mobile phone.

***

The night sky was filled with a billion stars, bright enough to allow Tracker to see his way safely over the rocks and cracks atop the gorge. He spotted the faint light radiating from a cave high up on the gorge wall and pointed it out to Ryan.

"He made it to the cave. Lots of places to hide in there."

"Won't matter, though, you'll still be able to track him. Won't you?"

"Yeah. But he's crafty; might set some traps for us. Have to be careful."

Tracker stepped to the very edge of the gorge and searched over the rock wall, soon locating Donna, the beam from her flashlight jerking erratically as she made her way along the narrow, uneven path. Tracker sat on a rock while Ryan stood at the edge, waiting for her to make it to the top. When she was within arm's reach, Ryan stretched his hand out to help her up. Watching them, Tracker thought about how easy it would be to give Ryan a nudge and send the two of them to their deaths. Two cops with one kick. As Donna put a foot onto the flat rock, she looked up and caught a glimpse of Tracker with a strange smile on his face.

***

The young cop raised the can of beer to his mouth, but before he could take a swig, it was knocked out of his hand, spilling on the ground. He turned to see Sgt. Watson glaring at him. "You're still on the job," Watson said. "Get plenty of food into you, but no booze." He walked around the campsite, making sure no one else was drinking. He turned to Constable Marsh. "Get on the radio to Derby, find out where that chopper is," he said, and Marsh got busy.

The satellite phone on Watson's belt rang, surprising him. He checked the caller ID, then answered. "Where have you been?"

"I'm at Kris's house, handcuffed to a pipe," came Bateman's reply.

"Come again?"

"That lawyer, McLaren, he's with Kris. In Creed."

"Our Kris? Kris Somers?"

"Yeah, she's in all the way with him."

"How do you know?"

"Coz he beat me over the fucking head with a cricket bat and they took off together."

Not long after, a squad car arrived at Kris's house, and a cop uncuffed Bateman. He went directly to the police station and issued himself another handgun and several magazines of ammunition.

***

At the Baudin Hotel, the clerk wound through video footage on the computer, soon finding vision of Sgt. Watson and Rooke meeting outside the Nicholls Room, Rooke carrying a briefcase.

"Is that Rooke?" Kris asked.

Tom nodded. "Yeah, that's him."

On the screen, Rooke and Sgt. Watson entered the room. The clerk fast-forwarded the footage, and soon Sgt.

Watson emerged, carrying the briefcase.

"Clearly an exchange has been made. You said there was another meeting?"

"Yes, just a moment."

The clerk wound back the video and found footage of Rooke greeting a man, face hidden by a panama hat, who was also carrying a briefcase. They walked into the Nicholls Room.

"Any idea who that is?" Kris asked. Tom shook his head. The clerk fast-forwarded some more, and the mystery man left without the briefcase.

"So he left the briefcase with Rooke, who handed it to Sgt. Watson."

"We need to identify this guy," Tom said to the clerk. "Did you get a look at him?"

"I don't recall, we get a lot of people coming through our doors."

"Do you mind?" Tom asked, gesturing at the controls.

"Not at all."

Tom wound the tape back, pausing at the mystery man as he looked at his watch, face still concealed by the panama hat. "Well, that's something, I guess."

"He's checking the time, so what?"

"He wears his watch on his right hand, on the inside of his wrist. Unusual combination, don't you think? And that looks like an authentic panama hat, not a cheap knock-off."

"Can you make me a copy?" Kris asked, and pulled a thumb drive from her keys. She handed it to the clerk, and he inserted it into the computer and started copying the vision.

Tom noticed a police car pulling up across the street from the hotel. With a glance and a nod, he notified Kris as the save operation on the computer continued.

"Is there a rear exit?"

"Just over there," the clerk said, pointing out another door. Kris and Tom kept their eyes on the two cops, who got out of the police car and separated. One of them headed across the street towards the hotel.

The save completed and Kris whipped the thumb drive from the computer. "Thanks," she said, and they hurried out through the back door.

Tom and Kris legged it to her police car and got in as sirens sounded nearby. She drove away from the kerb.

"They've just left the hotel," a cop said over the radio. "Looking for a female police officer and a white male in a Hawaiian shirt and a fedora hat."

"Roger that," said another cop.

"Aw shit," Kris said.

A police car entered the road a few blocks ahead, lights flashing. She turned down a side street and accelerated down a sloping laneway, turned down another laneway past some derelict houses and spun into a vacant lot. The headlights beamed over piles of discarded furniture and other junk. There was some movement amongst it, people reacting to the headlights and scrambling out of sight. She shut off the lights and engine.

"We'll be safe here for a while," she said.

Tom could see silhouetted people stirring in the

shadows. "What is this place?"

"It's a hang-out for junkies. They won't bother us."

"You know, I have a good idea where Konnigan is. I think I could get her to talk, confess to the whole business. Make it all stop," he said.

"Just like that? All the time and money invested in this, and she's just going to stop?"

"She's probably got no idea about most of this. She looks at the big picture; delegates the details to people like Rooke."

"Just coz she doesn't want to know, doesn't make her innocent."

"Of course. But she's no murderer. If I can just explain to her—"

"There are cops everywhere."

"Looking for a female cop and a guy in a fedora and a Hawaiian shirt. It's worth a shot."

Kris got out and opened the trunk, pulling out an electronic contraption. The murmurs and whispers coming from the surrounding shadows made her uncomfortable, but she calmly closed the trunk and got back in the car, where Tom had removed his shirt. She taped the surveillance wire to his chest, put on the headphones and tested the volume levels, making adjustments.

"How do you know she'll be there?"

"She's a barfly. She'll be plastered by now. She might even be willing to spill her guts."

"Or Rooke might spill yours. If you get spooked, move into the crowd and get out of there," she said. He nodded.

"Are you absolutely sure you want to do this?"

"Yeah. Let's do it."

He put on the koala shirt and the baseball cap, and they got out. Kris shone her flashlight onto some of the junkies nearby. "Who wants to make fifty bucks?"

"What do I gotta do?" a man called back.

"I need a woman."

"That's fucking discrimination," the man called back.

"I can help you out there, honey," a woman said. Kris swung her flashlight over to the voice and found its owner: a sleazy young woman who looked like she was no stranger to the local STD clinic. She walked over.

"All right, you know where the Old Pearl Hotel is?" Kris asked.

"I sure do. I'm Jo, by the way, nice to meet you."

"Hi Jo, I want you to walk my friend to the hotel, can you do that?"

"For fifty bucks, I can blow him right here," she said, approaching. "We don't need a hotel."

"It's fifty bucks to take a walk, that's all." Kris handed her the cash. "You get some more when you finish the job."

"No worries," Jo said, putting an arm around Tom. He was immediately overwhelmed by her repulsive odour and slipped out of her embrace. "That won't be necessary," he said.

She shrugged. "Not the romantic type, huh?" she said, breathing into his face.

"It's a classy place, so . . ." Kris sprayed a bottle of perfume at the woman.

Tom was grateful for the gesture, but thought the whole bottle wouldn't be enough to mask the stench.

"Good luck," Kris said.

Tom nodded and walked towards the dark laneway with his new companion.

"What about you, girl?" someone called from the shadows. "You need something?"

"No, thank you," Kris said, and got back into the car, locking the doors.

***

Music spilled out from bars along the street, and Tom and Jo blended in with the crowd. He kept the baseball cap tilted over one eye and put his arm around Jo as a police car passed, the cop scouring the crowd but not giving him a second look. They approached the Old Pearl Hotel, and Tom pulled Jo close as they entered. They walked through the lobby to the bar entrance, which was guarded by two Maori security guards, their faces tattooed Maori style, muscles stacked on their massive frames. Judging by the disapproving way they looked at Jo, Tom thought it best to leave her outside.

"Thanks, I'll take it from here," Tom said, and handed her some money.

"I'm coming in for a drink."

"Not with me."

"Fuck you, you arrogant prick!"

Tom walked inside the bar, which was about half-full; a small crowd gathered around a pianist who was singing a jazz number in the corner. No sign of Konnigan. He wandered among the patrons and spotted Rooke sitting on a lounge chair, looking right back at him, sipping his drink. Rooke smiled and nodded a greeting. Tom reciprocated, wondering if Rooke knew anything about recent events, or if Watson had kept the manhunt quiet for now.

The cell phone in Tom's pocket rang, and he picked up, keeping an eye on Rooke, who was still watching him.

"Hello," Tom said.

"This is Hannah Wright, I got a missed call from this number."

"Hannah, yes. This is Tom McLaren, you gave me your card."

"Oh, hi," she said.

"This is a bad time, I'll call you back."

"Okay, no prob—"

He ended the call as Rooke pointed across the room to the crowd around the piano. Tom soon realised Konnigan was the pianist. He strolled up beside her, and she smiled, pleasantly surprised to see him. She finished the tune to a round of applause. "Thank you, I'll take a short break," she said, and stood up. "How the heck are you, Tom?"

"I'm alive."

"Ha! Well, life is a lot better with a drink in your hand, come on, my shout." They stepped over to the bar, where Konnigan showed the barman two fingers, and he went about fixing two whiskeys. Tom's mind was racing. He'd been too busy focusing on evading the police to actually consider what he was going to say to Konnigan, who wasn't as loaded with booze as he would have liked.

Still nursing his drink, Rooke kept an eye on them and discreetly took out his mobile phone. He connected some earphones and dialled a number.

The mobile phone in Konnigan's handbag lit up in activation without a sound. She didn't notice and neither did Tom.

"What happened to your camping trip?" she asked.

"Let's see, Ed's missing, and Anthony died from a snakebite."

Konnigan laughed raucously, taking a mouthful of whiskey, then realised Tom wasn't laughing. "You're not joking."

"Why didn't you tell us what you were up to?"

Rooke put his drink down and pushed the earphone deeper into his ear.

"What? What are you talking about?" Konnigan asked.

"I'm talking about your dirty deeds to get the land lease. We're your lawyers, Dawn, you should've come to us first. You should've trusted us."

***

Kris sat quietly in the squad car, also tuned in to the conversation, headphones pressed tightly against her head. A junkie appeared outside her window, tapping against the glass. Kris ignored him and concentrated on the audio.

***

"Would you stop this nonsense and tell me the facts? No speculation, no assumptions. Tell me what the hell happened and why you think *I* was involved. The facts, please!" Konnigan said.

"The local police were paid seventy grand. That's a fact. Here's another fact: the local cops kidnapped Abe Whitaker's grandson. Any of this ring a bell?"

"No. It doesn't."

"Cut the bullshit and tell me straight. You masterminded some conspiracy here to get your hands on the lease."

"What?" she said, then laughed mirthlessly. She turned to face Tom directly and looked him straight in the eye. "Are you out of your tiny fucking mind? That uranium mine represents about six percent of QPEC's leases worldwide. Do you think I'd commit federal crimes for that?"

"Yes, I do. You're accustomed to getting your way, Dawn. That's why you hired a guy like Rooke."

***

Kris suddenly became aware that the car was surrounded by several junkies. She took the car's radio handpiece and put it to use. "Step away from the vehicle," she said, her voice booming through the speakers on the car roof.

The passenger window smashed inwards and Kris unclipped the Taser from her belt. A hand leaned in and unlocked the rear door, and before she knew it, there were three junkies swarming inside. She Tasered one of them, but he was quickly replaced by another. They overpowered her and dragged her out of the vehicle and onto the dirt.

She fought back, but there were too many, and she was soon helpless, her shirt ripped open.

Then the place was filled with flashing blue lights and blaring sirens, and the junkies scrambled for cover. Kris, on her knees, looked up to see Bateman getting out of the police car, gun in hand.

"In a spot of trouble, Kris?"

***

Konnigan downed her drink. "All right, the truth is I paid a couple of local cops to rough up a few Aboriginals. But there was no kidnapping or extortion."

"You paid the cops a seventy grand to rough up the locals?"

"Don't be ridiculous. It was two grand, not a cent more. If there's been kidnapping, I'll pack up and pull out. On my word." Tom looked her in the eye and was leaning towards believing her. "Christ," she said, "if it is true, I've got a good idea who's behind it."

Rooke reacted to Konnigan's words, abruptly pocketing his phone. He took out a vial and carefully emptied its liquid contents into his drink, stirring it with the straw.

"I'm not squeaky clean, never claimed to be," Konnigan continued, "but I've never been involved in any kidnapping, Tom. On my word."

"Hope you don't mind if I join you," Rooke said, approaching.

"Send your goon away," Tom said.

"Don't worry about Rooke, he's harmless," she said.

Tom looked at Rooke, and it crossed his mind that perhaps Rooke had acted independently of Konnigan. She certainly seemed genuinely surprised by Tom's revelations.

"We're busy, Rooke, take a walk," she said. Rooke smiled, then splashed his drink on Konnigan's chest. "For fuck's sake, man!" she said, then grabbed Rooke's collar like she was going to throttle him. He pushed away from her, and she began gasping and choking, her face turning blue.

"Easy," Rooke said, as she collapsed to the floor.

"Doctor!" Tom yelled. "Is there a doctor here?!"

"Quiet now," Rooke said, and Tom noticed the palm-sized handgun he was holding. "Walk out," Rooke said.

Tom did as he was told, Rooke escorting him towards the exit with the gun inconspicuously held against his back. As a crowd gathered around Konnigan, Tom considered his options: complying would most certainly end in his death, probably in the nearest back alley. He had to find a way to disarm Rooke, at least temporarily, so he could escape. As they approached the two Maori bouncers at the door, Tom noticed an empty table a few steps ahead with some beer bottles sitting unattended. As Rooke and Tom passed the table, Tom discreetly lifted a half-empty beer bottle and hid it under his untucked shirt. They were right at the door when one of the bouncers put a huge open palm on Tom's chest.

"You can't take that with you," the bouncer said, and Tom put the beer down on a nearby table. "What have you got there, mate?" the bouncer asked, referring to the hand Rooke was holding behind Tom's back.

Rooke swung his pistol around in plain sight. "Step back," Rooke said, and the Maoris complied. Before Rooke could point the gun back at him, Tom grabbed Rooke's hands and tried to wrestle the weapon from him. The bouncers jumped in, all hands going for the gun. A shot was fired, and one of the bouncers reeled backwards, blood pouring from his leg. People yelled and screamed, rushing for the exits; panic and pandemonium ensued.

The other Maori wrestled Rooke to the ground, and Tom took the opportunity to flee, bolting through the exit with the crowd and through the busy lobby.

Rooke jabbed the Maori in the throat, leaving him choking as he rolled from beneath him with the gun in his hand, the other bouncer cowering out of his way and clutching his bloody leg. Rooke stormed out.

Dozens of patrons, Tom among them, ran out of The Old Pearl onto the street.

"Tom McLaren!" a voice called.

Tom turned and saw a cop reaching for his handgun. A big, heavy guy pushed past, and Tom tapped the guy's ankle and sent him tripping up into the cop, both of them going to ground. Tom fled through the sprawling patrons.

The beach was busy, floodlights shining over hundreds of people enjoying the still, balmy night. Tom walked casually onto the sand, doing his best to blend in with the other beachgoers. He turned and saw the three cops had spotted him and were sprinting towards him.

Tom bolted off the soft sand, weaving through people, and onto the firmer, wet sand at the water's edge. He figured that when he'd run far enough, he would run back up onto the road parallel to the beach, which was teeming with pedestrians.

A car horn blasted repeatedly, and dozens of people poured onto the beach in a panic. Sirens blaring, a police car emerged and drove onto the soft sand, speeding towards Tom. But it soon bogged to a standstill, rear wheels spinning up a storm of white sand.

Rooke's handgun was holstered to his ankle beneath the leg of his pants when he raced onto the beach. He quickly spotted Tom fleeing from the police.

A group of youths on the soft sand were sitting around a bonfire, smoking weed and drinking booze, oblivious to the manhunt going on nearby. As Tom ran by them, he boosted one of their surfboards. One of the guys got up to give chase, but when he noticed the three cops racing towards him, his priority shifted to hiding the bag of weed that was lying in the open. He chucked a towel over it just as the three cops tore through the group in pursuit.

Tom ran into the water, hurdling a couple of waves before jumping chest down onto the board. Keeping low, he cut through the waves and paddled straight out into the dark water. When he had gone far enough to be out of sight from the beach, he rested on one shoulder and looked behind him. There were about a half-dozen cops gathered at the water's edge, two off-road police vehicles arriving. But judging by the way they held their flashlights out in different directions, he was sure they couldn't see him. He took a moment to catch his breath, then set off parallel to the shore.

Some of the cops were searching with binoculars while others kept the crowd at bay. One of the cops had Sgt. Watson on the radio and, having explained the situation to him, was told to contact an officer who was in charge of the police boat. The young man explained that the cop in question was off-duty and had a prior engagement.

"I don't give a flying fuck about his wife's birthday, we need that boat on the water now!" Watson yelled, and the young officer knew better than to argue.

"Yessir!"

***

Claire stood on the balcony of her hotel room, watching the commotion on the street and beach below.

"What on earth is going on here? I thought you said this was a sleepy little town?" she said.

"It's supposed to be," Drake said, joining her on the balcony.

"Looks like a police pursuit," said Claire.

"Probably just a bag snatcher."

"No. There's something big going down."

"You're perfectly safe here, ma'am," Drake said, then went back inside and checked the door to the suite, relieved to see there were two security guards on duty.

***

On a runabout boat tied to the jetty, a crusty young fisherman was packing up gear, ready to disembark when

Rooke dropped down onto the rear deck. The young man, tall and powerfully built, stood and turned towards him, towering over Rooke. "What's on your mind?"

"My brother was swimming," Rooke said, "he got caught in a rip. Would you mind searching for him in your boat?"

"It's not my boat," the young man said. The skipper, a middle-aged man with a greying mullet, stepped out from the cabin.

"What the hell's he doing swimming at this time o' night? Been drinkin'?" the older guy asked.

"Yeah, had a little too much to drink."

"All right, then, better get a wriggle on, then."

With that, the young man cast them off while the other started the engine and pulled the boat away from the jetty. "Whereabouts is he?"

***

Tom paddled along, keeping an eye on the beach activity as he headed along the coast. The sound of the runabout's engine carried over the water, and he turned to see the light from the boat bouncing over the waves in his direction. He turned out to sea, but only took a few strokes before he struck something solid that grated on the underside of the board. He knew it was a reef.

***

The sonar equipment was beeping repeatedly.

"The reef's just up ahead," the skipper said, easing the

throttle. Rooke stood beside him and leaned over the windscreen, aiming the searchlight out in front. The younger man stood portside, keeping an eye out for the reef and the swollen body of a drowned swimmer.

"He might be clinging to it. Let's get closer," Rooke said. The skipper pivoted the boat, and they scooted closer to the reef, the equipment going berserk now. "Shut that thing off," Rooke said.

"Don't start giving orders, mate," the skipper said.

Rooke reached down to his ankle and came back up with the handgun. He leaned forward on the windscreen, eyes still on the water. "Shut it off."

The skipper promptly switched off the equipment and looked over to his friend, who was gawking at the gun. Rooke listened carefully and soon heard the sound of the grating surfboard. He swept the light over the water and found the surfboard bobbing up and down on the reef. No sign of Tom.

Beneath the waves, clinging to the reef, Tom raised his head, face first, and breached the surface with his lips. He exhaled slowly, careful not to make a lot of noise. He took a breath and sank below the surface again, holding his breath as the light passed over the water just above him. He stayed under as long as he could, then went back up to the surface and exhaled slowly, trying to minimise noise. As he slowly inhaled, a wave washed over him, and he took in a mouthful of water, forcing him to burst out of the sea in a coughing fit.

Rooke swung the light around and found his target. Before

he could take a shot, Tom ducked into the water. Rooke waited, listening for almost a minute before he heard a gentle swoosh of water. He spun the light to the left, catching Tom resurfacing. Rooke took a shot as Tom dived out of sight.

He took a gaff hook and handed it to the young guy. "Go get him."

"What do you mean?"

Rooke held the gun to the skipper's head. "He's hiding behind the reef over there. Bring him in. One way or another."

Lying on his stomach, hugging the reef, Tom watched the man climb out of the boat with a flashlight and the gaff hook, while Rooke pointed the gun at the skipper.

"Don't come back without him," Rooke said. The man wobbled over the reef and Tom went under again. The man heard the slight splash and shot the light over to catch sight of Tom's shoulder as he dipped into the water.

Tom sat at the bottom of the reef pool, clinging to spongy reef plants to keep him from floating. He looked up at the glassy surface glittering in the moonlight, and guessed he could hold on for about a minute and a half. Then a powerful beam of light shone through nearby, lighting up the reef around him, the reeds swaying gently in the current. The light moved slowly towards him, carefully scanning. There was nowhere for him to go. All he could do was hope it would pass over him. But it found him, and it fixed right onto his face, blinding him. Then he felt the gaff hook prodding his leg.

Tom stood up in the waist-deep water, the man

standing over him, flashlight pointed at his chest.

"Come on," the young guy said. "Head over to the boat."

Tom looked up at the guy, silhouetted by the searchlight coming from the boat. Tom stayed behind his shadow to stop the gunman on the boat from getting a clear shot.

"Give me a hand, will you?" Tom said, stretching out his right hand. The guy offered him the end of the gaff hook. He took hold and the guy pulled him up. Tom lunged forward, using the guy's momentum to push him backwards into a rocky pool, Tom diving beside the falling man as a gunshot rang out. The guy floundered beside him, the flashlight briefly illuminating the reef around Tom, giving him a quick view of a channel through the reef. He thrust himself forwards and paddled like hell.

"Get us closer!" Rooke yelled through gritted teeth, taking the searchlight from the older guy still sitting at the controls. Rooke leaned over the portside, light held over handgun as he scanned the water. The skipper accelerated abruptly and pulled a hard turn, flipping Rooke out of the boat. As he went under, the boat sped to the side of the reef near the younger guy, who grabbed the diving platform at the rear.

"Go! Go! Go!" the young guy yelled, and the skipper obliged, the boat disappearing over the dark water.

Now on the opposite side of the reef, Tom peered over and watched the silhouetted man claw his way up. The man stood poised with a gun in firing position, scanning the area. Since the gunman was dressed in a soaking suit, Tom thought it had to be Rooke. He gently pushed himself away from the reef, into the open water.

Chapter 28

"Take a right here," Bateman said, and Kris turned off the highway onto a gravel road. Kris grimaced as Bateman rested an elbow on the shoulder of her seat, his stinking, sweaty armpit uncomfortably close. In his other hand was a Glock handgun, which he held loosely on his lap, pointed at her.

"We were all right, you and me. Never had a problem or nothin'. Am I right?"

"Right."

"So why'd you have to come humbuggin' and ruin everything?"

"I was doing my job."

"Your job was to capture the cop-killer."

"That's exactly what I did. But you know as well as I do, he'd have Buckley's of getting to the magistrate in one piece," Kris said.

"So you broke ranks and took him back to your joint. Did you fuck him?"

She grimaced again in disbelief. "No."

"So what the fuck did you go against all of us for?"

"I told you, I was doing my job."

"Yeah, well, that was a big fucken mistake, acting all high and righteous. We gotta stick together out here. You know that!"

"What now?" she said, though she didn't need him to answer. They were headed deep into the bush and his intentions were crystal clear.

"Yep, what now," he said, and pulled his gun hand close to her head, but only to scratch his red, chafed forearm.

Chapter 29

Sgt. Watson stood in the clearing, waving a flashlight at the approaching lights in the night sky. His men had long packed up and headed back to their vehicles. The helicopter descended, and he guided them down to a relatively flat patch of spinifex. The passenger door swung open, and Watson ducked as he ran beneath the blades and climbed inside. The pilot shot him a smile, handed him a headset, and then lifted off at great speed and headed for the distant lights of Creed. Watson was grateful that the pilot didn't ask him anything other than whether he thought the suspect was armed, which he answered in the affirmative. It was one thing to explain to his men that they were after a cop-killer; it was another to explain to a cop from out of town. He was still working on his official explanation for his daughter and Piper being on a cliff top with a civilian in remote bushland.

"With a bit of luck, we'll beat *that*," the pilot said, pointing to a screen showing satellite imagery of a large storm system headed their way.

In a matter of minutes, they were cruising over the beach

approaching the town, scanning the waters for the suspect, who was last seen on a surfboard. The chopper was equipped with thermal imagery and a powerful spotlight, and they employed both. They soon spotted a figure swimming towards a deserted beach and hovered above him, the powerful searchlight locking onto him. He stopped paddling, seemingly exhausted and resigned to his fate. This puzzled Watson—why would the guy just give up? Another eighty, maybe a hundred strokes and he'd be on the beach, where he could at least make a dash for the trees. With their equipment, they'd still find him, but that never stopped a felon from attempting to flee. He looked long and hard at the familiar-looking man treading water. Then his lips parted in surprise: the man in the water was Rooke. As the lights of the police boat bounced over the surf towards Rooke, Watson told the pilot to drop him at the jetty where the police boat would soon be heading.

***

It was raining, and lightning flashed over the sea on the horizon as the storm rolled in towards Creed. Watson stood on the pontoon of the jetty and watched as the two officers secured the police boat and Rooke climbed out. Watson told the two officers he would take care of the paperwork, and they were glad to be relieved of it; they were even gladder to be relieved of duty for the night. "No sense going back out in this shit," Watson said. "Just leave the keys in the boat; I'll take her out myself when this blows over."

"Righto, Watto," said the skipper. "Keys are hooked up behind the dash."

"Goodo."

"I hope you find this prick."

"We'll get him," Watson said, and he and Rooke stayed and watched as the young officers climbed up the ladder to the jetty and jogged towards the beach as the storm drew closer.

"What the hell were you doing out there?" Watson asked.

"I was doing your job," Rooke said.

"How's that?"

"I know all about it. Your man got made by three fucking lawyers on a camping trip. The same lawyers who work for my employer."

"It was just rotten luck, nobody's fault," said Watson, trying not to sound sheepish.

"Now it's a fucking fiasco," said Rooke.

"It's not as bad as all that."

"You've got a small army of cops trying to track down one of the lawyers; one dead lawyer; one dead cop. It's a goddamned shit-slingin' shindig, wall-to-fucking-wall; and now *I've* got my hands dirty."

"So you got him?"

"I think I clipped him."

"You *think*?"

"I can't be certain. Either way, he's within two clicks of the reef. You need two or three cops patrolling the beach on quad bikes; send everyone else home."

"I've already done that," said Watson.

"What about the job I paid you for? Have you done that?"

"We got two signatures, still need the old man's."

"And the boy?"

"He got loose somehow," Watson said. Rooke stared blankly at him, an expression Watson had seen before on mugshots of sociopaths. "He's not going anywhere," Watson said. "He's trapped in a cave up in the gorge. We'll have him soon enough."

"Just how many cops know about our little project?"

"Five. Five good cops. One of them's dead, so four. We've had a few snags, but this was never going to be easy," Watson said.

Rooke gave him another blank look.

"She'll be right, we'll get it done," Watson said.

"I know. I'll make sure of it."

They climbed the ladder to the jetty and walked towards the shore.

In the darkness beneath the jetty, Tom lay on the surfboard, clinging to the timber pilings. He had heard the entire conversation above. He had heard where the keys to the boat were kept.

Tom stayed put as the storm struck, lashing the jetty in a torrential downpour. The police boat and the pontoon rocked violently with the waves, the boat bouncing off the rubber fenders. The way Tom saw it, the boat was his best chance of escaping alive. He could use it to get to the closest major town, Derby, where he could contact everybody he knew, as well as the media, before turning himself in to local authorities. But he would have to act before the storm was over; before Watson returned to resume the search with the boat.

He climbed onto the boat, slid a hand behind the dash and felt around, soon finding the keys hanging on a hook, just as the young cop had said. As the boat seesawed with the waves, rain still pouring down, he turned the key and started the powerful twin engines. The navigation display came on automatically, and he figured his way around it, setting his course to Derby.

He stepped away from the controls to cast off the ropes, when a powerful wave forced the boat against the rubber fenders. He clung to the railing, noticing an acute pain in his index finger. The boat steadied, and he looked at his blackened finger with half the nail missing, courtesy of David. The memory of the child pulling off his nail made him smile briefly, then worry that the boy wasn't going to make it through the night. It dawned on him that even if he contacted outside police and they intervened, it was unlikely they would get to David before Watson and Rooke did. David may have been able to lose Watson in the caves last time, but now there would be Rooke and possibly others to contend with. Tom had no doubt that Rooke would see the job through.

Chapter 30

Kris drove the car into the clearing at the base of the cliff and saw that the paddy wagon containing Anthony's body was the only vehicle left. At gunpoint, she parked, got out and stood at the rear of the paddy wagon while Bateman opened the rear doors and shone a flashlight inside. Anthony's body was still there, rigid and cold.

"Now, where is the bloody thing? Woah!" Bateman jumped back as the furious taipan darted out onto the ground and made for the bush.

"Get in," Bateman said to Kris, "now!" She climbed inside and he locked the rear doors. Kris watched through the window as Bateman holstered his weapon, then limped after the snake. He soon caught up to the creature and grabbed it by the tail, holding it at arm's length. He hobbled back towards the car, but before he made it, the snake struck him suddenly, biting him on the cheek.

"Ahh! Slut!" he yelled, grabbing it around the neck.

Kris wriggled back away from the door as Bateman rushed towards the vehicle. He opened the rear door and hurled the snake inside, the animal sliding along the floor and stopping just in front of Kris. Bateman locked the door, and a moment later, Kris heard the roar of his engine as he sped away.

He drove one-handed, clutching his swelling cheek. He started foaming at the mouth and coughing, gasping for air, before he lost control of the car and it slid into a ditch, ramming into a mound of dirt. Still coughing, he tried to drive out. The wheels spun and the engine roared, but the car didn't move. He climbed out, still spluttering, and hurriedly examined the car, soon finding one of the rear tires bogged in the soft, red dirt. He crouched down, popped the valve cap and pressed on the valve. As the tire deflated, his face swelled. It was like the air was entering his body through his finger and filling in his red cheeks. He shuffled back behind the wheel, started the engine and floored it. He managed to drive the vehicle free, but only briefly before another wheel became bogged.

His face was black and purple and grotesquely swollen when he climbed out. He staggered around the car towards the trapped wheel, but fell to the ground, moaning and frothing severely from the mouth.

***

Kris eased out of her jacket as the snake raised its head in an aggressive pose. She held the jacket out in front of her, spread it wide open, then lunged at the animal, smothering it. It darted about beneath the fabric, and she felt her way to its head, its tail wriggling frantically. She crushed its neck with both hands as it thrashed some more, then finally went limp. She held on a while longer, then pulled her baton from her belt and rolled it over the head like a rolling pin, just to be sure. Kris lifted the jacket and, satisfied it was dead, she crawled to the door, only to find it locked.

Chapter 31

The bush and scrub outside the cave provided enough cover for Tracker to creep close enough so that he could peer inside without being seen. In the middle of the cave floor, he saw a deserted campfire. Ryan and Donna stood just behind Tracker.

"What are we hiding for?" Ryan whispered. "He's just a kid. What's he gonna do?"

Tracker studied the inside of the cave and didn't respond. Donna shrugged her shoulders at Ryan. He stepped out of the bush, branches rustling, and stepped towards the cave entrance. Before he could take a second step, something shot out from the cave and struck Ryan, sending him to the ground. He lay on his back with a spear sticking out of his shoulder. Donna snatched her firearm from its holster, stepped out and fired blindly three times into the cave before helping Ryan to his feet. She fired again, pulled him deep into the bushes and set him down on his side. He moaned, clutching at the spear. As she examined the wound, Tracker stormed up beside them and whipped the spear out in one swift motion. Ryan groaned in agony, then fell flat on his back.

Chapter 32

It was still raining when Tom jumped the fence, walked past the empty pool and into the rear entry of the hotel, his clothes soaking wet. There were a few people wandering around the lobby. He walked past the breakfast bar where he and his colleagues had met Konnigan for brunch, then took the elevator up to the penthouse. He stepped out to see two bodyguards on duty outside Claire's room. He composed himself and approached with a smile.

"I don't think so, move along," one of the men said.

"Tell her Tom's here. Tom McLaren."

"Sir, I'm asking you politely."

"Claire!" he yelled. "Claire, it's Tom!"

The bodyguards grabbed hold of him, and he struggled as they dragged him down the corridor. One of them hit the elevator button, and they shoved his face against the wall, waiting for the elevator to arrive.

The door to the room opened, and Drake appeared, Claire standing behind her. "It's okay, he's a friend," Drake said. They unhanded Tom and stepped aside, apologising profusely.

***

Drake sipped her tea while Claire sat transfixed as Tom explained the nightmare that had unfolded over the last two days.

"Are you suggesting that the local police are responsible?" Claire asked.

"Some of them are definitely involved. You need to bring in the federal police."

"The normal procedure is to contact local authorities," Claire said. "I understand the complexities here, but I don't have the authority to override police procedure."

"Of course you do!" Tom said. "You make a phone call and the tactical response team arrives in no time! How much authority do you need?"

"Tom, you don't understand the bureaucracy, I don't have that much power."

"Yes, you do," Drake said. "You've got a federal contact who can take care of the red tape. I'll organise it."

"Thank you," Tom said, leaning back in his armchair. Drake took out her mobile phone and made a call. Drake listened for a moment, then appeared to have not received a response. She hung up and tried again.

Claire smiled at Tom and he forced a smile back. He was bothered by her apparent reluctance to help and turned away from her, eyes wandering over the room. He noticed a white hat on a stand by the door and looked at it curiously. It was a panama and it looked familiar. Then he remembered the CCTV footage from the hotel. He looked hard at Drake; could she be the mystery person in the panama? Same build, he thought. Same kind of suit. Was she wearing a watch on her right wrist? He glanced over and saw Drake was wearing something on her right wrist but, half-covered by the sleeve of her shirt, it could have been a bracelet.

"What time is it?" he asked. At that, Drake raised her right hand, revealing the watch face on the inside of her wrist.

"Twenty past nine," she said.

Tom stood up and walked to the stand, taking the hat and examining it. "Nice hat," he said to Claire. "Yours?"

"It's mine," Drake said. "Put it back, please."

Tom replaced the hat, and Drake turned her back on him and dialled a number on her phone again. From behind, with her short hair and strong build, Tom was no longer in any doubt. Drake was a key player in the conspiracy; Claire may have been too. He thought they most likely misappropriated state government money to finance their scheme. *But how did they get Rooke involved?* Then he remembered some of the news stories about Rooke, a former government bodyguard.

"You need to come to the hotel," Drake said into the phone.

Tom looked to the door, then to the balcony window, and wondered how far he would get if he ran. He noticed a mobile phone charging on the kitchen bench.

"Can I use your phone?" he asked Claire. "I gotta try to reach Ed."

"Yes, of course," she said, pointing to the phone on the bench. "Five, three, seven, four is the code."

Tom walked into the kitchen, took out his wallet and found Hannah's card. Keeping an eye on Claire and Drake, he used the phone to make a video call to Hannah. He placed the phone on the bench, the camera lens turned towards Claire and Drake.

***

In her hotel room, Hannah accepted the video call. She soon recognised Premier Claire Bosworth on the screen, who seemed unaware she was on camera. Hannah scrambled to activate the recording feature on her phone.

***

Tom walked back to the lounge and noticed Drake shooting Claire a private look. Claire turned to Tom. "You must be famished, can I order you something to eat?"

"What have you got in your minibar?" Tom asked, opening the refrigerator. He grabbed a pack of crisps, a chocolate bar and a beer, placing them on the bar. Starving, he ripped open the crisps and tucked into them, washing them down with the beer, which he soon finished.

"Is it Rooke?" Tom said. "Is that who you sent for?"

"I beg your pardon?"

"Lewis Rooke," Tom said. "Konnigan's driver. He held a gun in my back earlier on."

"What? Wasn't it the police who—?"

"Yeah, but Rooke's your middleman. He paid off the cops.

Seventy grand, wasn't it? To intimidate and brutalise the local indigenous people, and kidnap the boy."

"That's absurd!" Drake said.

"The money was in that briefcase you handed him at the Baudin Hotel. In the Nicholls Room, about ten thirty Wednesday morning. You wore the panama. There were video cameras in the hotel."

"I knew nothing about any kidnapping!" Claire said.

"Quiet, Claire!" said Drake, in an officious tone that surprised Tom. "Neither of us knows about any kidnapping."

"Not the details, maybe, but you didn't pay the cops seventy grand for speeding tickets."

"Security," Drake called calmly, like she was calling a dog. In seconds, the two heavies were standing inside the doorway, awaiting her command. "Restrain him," she said, and they immediately shoved his face against the wall, twisted his arms behind his back and bound them with a plastic hand tie. Drake took out her phone, walked out of the suite and shut the door.

***

The Mercedes cruised along the highway back to Creed. Behind the tinted windows, Rooke sat behind the wheel, an illuminated mobile phone sitting on the console.

"The Nicholls Room. Their surveillance equipment."

"Why the Baudin Hotel?" asked Watson, his voice booming out of the phone's speaker.

"Why the question? Can you do it or do you need me to do it?" Rooke asked.

"Fuck you! It's done," said Watson, ending the call.

A short while later, the clerk at the reception of the Baudin Hotel stood back and watched as Sgt. Watson dismantled the hotel's computers.

"This is going to send us into chaos, you realise. How am I supposed to take bookings? How am I supposed to check people in and out?"

"Pen and paper," Watson said. "You can write, can't you?"

Watson hauled the computers out to his squad car, parked in front of the entrance. As he dumped them on the passenger seat, Donna's voice came over the radio.

"Bravo Whiskey to Papa," Donna called.

"Christ, what now?" Watson said as he walked around to the driver's side and got in.

"Bravo Whiskey to Papa, please come in!"

"Papa here, go ahead, Bravo Whiskey."

"We need to medevac Ryan out. He's hurt."

"What's he done?"

"He's been speared in the shoulder."

"Speared?"

"Yeah, old Abo chucked a spear at him, went straight through, it's pretty nasty. Deep wound."

Sgt. Watson sighed and took a moment. "Have you bandaged it up?"

"Yeah, but he needs a doctor."

"Can he walk?"

"I suppose he could."

"Good. So he stays until we finish the thing. What

about Tracker, he still with you?"

"Yeah, he's still here."

"Good, so set him loose. This is right up his alley. He can do whatever he needs to do to wrap it all up. You got that? It has got to be completed tonight."

"No worries. It'll get done."

"Have you heard from Bateman?" Watson asked.

"No, why?"

"I can't get a hold of him. I need you to go to point alpha, I'm pretty sure he's there, wrapping up some other business. Tell him Kris Somers has got a computer stick on her that needs to be destroyed, okay?"

"A what?"

"A computer thing with a video on it. I don't fucking know what it's called!"

"A USB?"

"Yeah, that's it! Needs to be destroyed. Got it?"

"Got it."

"Stay off the radio, I'll be up there soon."

***

Tom sat on the lounge in the hotel, hands behind his back. Claire sat beside him. Neither Drake nor the bodyguards were present. Tom glanced furtively at the mobile phone, which he hoped was still recording.

"I swear, I had no knowledge of any kidnapping," Claire said.

"You must've had an inkling," Tom said.

"I leave that kind of thing to Drake. She makes things

happen, I don't ask how. When things need to be done . . ." Claire said, but didn't finish.

"What? You step aside?"

"There are powerful people. You have no idea."

"You mean behind the scenes? Pulling the strings?" Tom asked. She didn't answer. "You were fucking me to keep tabs on the mining deal, weren't you?"

"No. That's not true," she said, then put her head in her hands.

"Was it their idea? These powerful people? Did they get us together so you could spy on me, keep track of the mining deal?"

"That's not why we met, but it was seen as an opportunity."

"By these powerful people? Who are they?"

"Families. Families who've been in the party for generations; they're . . . they're like dynasties of power brokers. You hardly ever see them, but they—I mean, I'm free to lead the party, but if I stray from their agenda, they 'correct' things. They make things . . ."

"Happen? Disappear?"

"That's all I'll say about it."

"And now they're going to make a little boy disappear, so they can push the mining deal through."

"I told you, I don't know anything about that."

"A child, Claire. They're going to murder a child."

She turned her back.

"Who are these people? Tell me their names."

The bodyguards walked in, and she walked out onto the balcony and closed the glass door.

"She told me all about it," Tom told the bodyguards.

"Quiet now," the shorter of the two men said.

"Conspiracy, kidnapping, extortion and murder. You blokes want to be a part of that?"

"I said be quiet."

"You're complicit in this too," Tom said.

The bigger guy punched Tom in the torso, buckling him over and knocking the wind out of him.

"You're gonna do time, both of you," he said, gasping for breath.

The two men exchanged looks, nodded, then began pummelling Tom, knocking him to the floor.

"That will do," Drake said, entering the room. Tom rolled onto his side, spitting out a mouthful of blood.

Drake stepped onto the balcony, sliding the door shut. "You're due to speak in less than an hour."

"I can't do it, not tonight," Claire said, and Drake realised she was crying.

Drake put both hands on her shoulders. "You can do it," she said. Claire shook her head.

"Don't let them kill the boy, Claire!" Tom yelled, so he could be heard outside the glass door. Drake signalled for the bodyguards to quieten Tom. One of them put a pillow to the floor and they both shoved his face into it.

"You can and you will!" Drake said, handing Claire a tissue. "Pull yourself together."

***

The two bodyguards escorted Tom out through the rear

entrance, the same way he had come in. One of his cheeks was black and blue and his lips were split. The black Mercedes sedan was parked nearby, rear door open. They shoved Tom inside, where he was pleased to discover Ed sitting beside him. He looked like he'd been in the wilderness for a week. They both smiled, each one filled with relief to see the other alive.

"You've looked better," Tom said.

"Me?" Ed laughed, eyes watering.

Tom looked over and saw Rooke sitting behind the wheel. Rooke turned and leaned towards Tom, holding a short blade in his hand. "Turn around."

Tom shuffled to one side and showed Rooke his tied hands. Rooke cut him free. He drove them away from the hotel.

"Did they rough you up?" Rooke asked. Tom ignored the comment. "I'm sorry about that. You're safe, now."

"You'll forgive my skepticism," Ed said.

"You can rest easy. We can't have the Premier knowingly involved in crime," Rooke said.

"I don't follow," Ed said.

"If we killed you, she'd be culpable. We have to keep her clean, which means keeping you alive. But you're not getting away clean. We have to implicate you. We'll fix it so there's undeniable proof you orchestrated the kidnapping."

"Impossible," said Ed.

"Actually, it's fairly simple and routine. We'll fabricate phone records, emails, bank accounts, hotel reservations, whatever it takes. You were as motivated as anyone to get that mining deal done."

"So we're going to prison?"

"You don't have to. You cooperate, and you both get to walk away from this big ugly mess. But there is one condition. You finish the job you came here to do." Rooke passed Ed a clipboard. Fastened to it was a contract, the QPEC Mining insignia on top. "Get the last signature. Shouldn't be too hard for you gents."

"What happens to the boy?"

"He'll be reunited with his father."

"And the grandfather?"

Rooke handed Tom a briefcase. "Open it," he said, and Tom did. Inside were dozens of stacks of hundred-dollar bills. "It comes tax free, with government authorisation. You comply, you get the dream. But if sometime down the track, either one of you gets a pang of conscience—even ten, twenty years from now—you'll both be implicated and killed before you can deny involvement. And your families will be culled like wild dogs."

"So we keep our mouths shut and we can just walk away?" Ed said.

"All the way down easy street," Rooke said.

"That's my kind of street," Tom said.

"How does that sit with you, sir?" Rooke asked Ed.

"Sounds more than reasonable."

***

Kris sat quietly in the back of the paddy wagon beside

Anthony's corpse and the dead snake. She noticed an approaching flashlight in the bush outside. She lay down on her back, playing dead, the baton held to her side. The footsteps drew closer, and soon a light shone inside the window, passing over the bodies and the dead snake. Finally, the door was unlocked and opened. A hand reached in, and two fingers were placed on Kris's neck, feeling for a pulse. Kris swung her baton upward and connected hard with the face.

Donna staggered backwards, straightened up and reached for her gun. Kris pounced, tackling her to the ground, but Donna soon had hold of her throat and thrust a knee into Kris's chest, taking the wind out of her. She pulled her handgun, but before she could aim, Kris wrapped both hands around it and twisted violently with a *SNAP!* breaking Donna's wrist and disarming her. She grabbed the gun and rammed the barrel under Donna's chin.

"Where's the boy?" Kris said.

"Fuck you!"

Kris planted a knee on Donna's broken wrist and she screamed in agony.

Chapter 33

Rooke drove up the winding gravel road lined by thick bush and trees. Tom's head was still throbbing from the beating he had taken. Ed looked utterly exhausted. They slowed to a halt, the headlights finding Sgt. Watson sitting on the hood of a police car, a rifle over his shoulder.

"Stay here," Rooke said, then got out and chatted with Sgt. Watson.

Tom watched them through the window, but couldn't make out what they were saying. He recognised that they were at the foothills before the caves.

Watson handed Rooke his rifle and approached Tom's door.

"For God's sake, Tom, get it signed," Ed said.

Watson opened the door and shone a light on their faces. "So nice to see you," he said. "Come on out; stretch your legs."

They got out and he gestured for them to head up the hill.

"Get it done," Rooke said, "then bring everybody down

here for debrief. I'll be waiting."

"Got it," Sgt. Watson said.

"I mean everybody," Rooke said.

Sgt. Watson nodded and walked Ed and Tom up through the bush with the flashlight. He had his handgun drawn in case either one attempted to flee into the dark.

Tom tried to ignore the aching stiffness in his limbs and his shoulders. How the hell was he going to get Abe to sign over the land? The man could not be bought for any amount of money. The only way Tom could see Abe signing was if someone held a gun to David's head. Tom was certainly not going to do that, but if he failed, he expected Rooke would, right after he killed Tom and Ed. So what was Tom to do?

The only thing you can do. Deal with whatever situation presents itself. Be open to opportunities, and above all, be ready to negotiate.

You don't really think Rooke intends to let you live, do you?

Why not? Ed seems to believe it.

Does he? Or is he simply willing himself to believe so he doesn't have to contemplate the horrific alternative? Even if we are allowed to walk free, what happens to David? Do they expect a kid to keep his mouth shut indefinitely?

None of it matters anyway. The old man isn't going to sign!

Deal with the circumstances. Be open to opportunities. That's all you can do.

They came to the cave mouth, a flickering light coming from within. Watson handed Tom a flashlight.

"You're up," Watson said. "Soon you'll hear a gunshot. That means you've got five minutes to come out with a done deal. The next shot you hear," he said, then pointed the handgun at Ed, "will be at the back of his head. Got it?"

Tom nodded and looked over to Ed, who appeared sorrier than ever. "No worries," Tom said, in the most cheerful tone he could manage. He winked at Ed, turned and walked inside the cave.

Clipboard in one hand, flashlight in the other, Tom walked in and saw the campfire in the middle of the floor. He shone the flashlight up to the natural balcony. No sign of anyone.

"David? It's Tom. You there?" He walked across the floor and into a passage and stood there for a moment, shining the light up to the bend. He had wandered about halfway up the passage when something sprung out in front of him: a rope, dangling from above. He looked up to see David's face sticking through a manhole. Tom tossed the clipboard up and the boy caught it. He pulled himself up the rope and David helped him into another passage. They walked around a corner and found Abe sitting behind a small campfire, looking back at them. Abe stood up and extended a hand, and Tom shook it.

"Thank you for helping my grandson."

"Didn't do him much good, I'm afraid," said Tom.

"You tried. What've you got there?"

Tom handed Abe the clipboard, and he looked over the contract, then looked at Tom; a long, searching look. Tom looked right back at him. "They sent me in here to get your signature."

"I'll die before I sign over the land," Abe said.

"That's what I thought," Tom said.

They looked each other in the eye, Tom's mind ticking over.

***

Ryan stood outside the cave mouth, Glock in one hand, radio in the other. His shoulder was wrapped in a blood-soaked bandage; his face was ashen. "Ryan here, Sarge. I got to get to a hospital."

"Hold tight, mate. Won't be long now."

"I lost a shitload of blood. I think I'm still bleeding," Ryan said. He was continuing to plead his case when Tom's voice called from inside the cave.

"I'm coming out," Tom called.

"Show me your hands!" Ryan said, holding up his weapon. He put the radio back on his belt and grabbed his flashlight, shining it into Tom's face. Tom walked out slowly, holding the clipboard above his head. "I'm unarmed. Mate, are you sure they haven't slipped past you?"

"They didn't slip past," Ryan said.

"I searched all over these caves, no sign of them," Tom said.

Ryan put the flashlight down and got back on the radio.

"Sarge, Ryan here. The lawyer fella's at my end. Reckons the Abos have shot through."

"So have they?" came Watson's gruff response.

"Shit no! Not at my end, anyway."

"Go in and take a look."

"Aw, come on, Sarge! I'm not faking, here!"

"Do you want to get this done or do you want to bleed to death?" Watson said.

"If I do, it's on you!" Ryan said and slammed the radio onto his belt.

"You don't look too good, mate. Isn't there someone else out here who could help?"

"Nah, it's just me now." He took his gun out again and waved Tom inside the cave. They shone their flashlights into every dark alcove they passed, and Ryan soon came upon a narrow passage that would have been easily missed.

"You been in there?" Ryan asked.

Tom shook his head. "Missed that one."

"Go on, then."

Ryan followed Tom slowly down the passage, the ceiling so low they had to duck. A distant gunshot rang out and Tom stopped for a moment.

"Tick-tock," Ryan said, and they continued.

***

Sgt. Watson and Ed waited outside the cave mouth. Ed looked terrible, his breathing laboured. Watson got on the radio. "What's going on, Ryan?" There was no answer. "Ryan! Come in!"

"All done," Ryan said over the radio.

"Thank Christ for that," Watson said.

"I'll send out the lawyer," Ryan said. A moment later, Tom emerged from the cave.

"Wasn't so hard, was it?" Watson asked. Tom walked up to Watson with the clipboard in his outstretched hand. Watson took it and, in doing so, revealed Ryan's handgun, which Tom had been holding beneath the clipboard.

"Get on the ground," Tom said, pointing the gun at Watson's face. Watson lowered himself onto his stomach. "Hands behind your head," Tom said, and Watson obeyed.

Inside the cave on the balcony, Ryan lay at Abe's feet, the old man holding the nulla-nulla to his throat. Ryan tried to speak, and Abe raised the weapon, threatening to strike. Then he shone the torch on Ryan's face, but got no reaction. His pupils did not dilate; his face a ghostly white, shirt soaked with blood. Abe lowered the weapon.

Ed fell to one knee, clutching his chest and groaning. Tom grabbed the pistol from Watson's holster and tossed it into the bushes. He raced to Ed's side and sat him down on a log. Watson stirred, and Tom saw he was going for a second handgun on his belt that Tom had missed.

"Don't!" Tom said, aiming the gun at him. Watson froze, and Tom walked over, took the handcuffs from Watson's belt, sunk a knee into his back and cuffed him. He looked over to Ed. "You okay, Ed?"

Ca-rack!

The gunshot sounded from down the hill, and echoed through the night sky. Ed fell lifelessly to the ground. Tom gasped, staring at the gaping hole in Ed's head. He hit the ground a split second before another shot was fired, the bullet smacking into rock and bouncing onto the ground in front of him. Tom could hear Rooke sprinting up through the underbrush towards him. He scrambled back into the cave.

"Hold your fire!" Watson called.

***

Tom raced across the chamber and up the passage towards Abe, who stood at the top, lighting the way with the flashlight.

Tom was almost at the top when Abe stumbled as a deafening blast filled the cave. Tom and David hit the floor while Abe clutched his bleeding chest. Tom aimed the Glock down into the chamber and fired a few rounds at the silhouetted figure in the entrance, as David dragged his grandfather around a corner.

"Go to the springs," Abe moaned, but David ignored him, trying to drag him further along. "No!" Abe said, pulling himself free. "Go to the springs. Then get back to our mob. I'll be okay. Just like before, remember?"

David nodded. Abe handed him the flashlight, looked into the boy's eyes and smiled, communicating a silent approval and confidence in the young man. Tears filled David's eyes and he smiled back at his grandfather.

Tom was squinting, gun pointing at the entrance. He couldn't see Rooke, wasn't sure if he had fled back out. He was startled by a tugging at his arm and turned to see David beckoning him. They ran down an adjoining passage into the bowels of the cave.

Chapter 34

Sgt. Watson crouched on the ground, hands still cuffed, as Rooke stepped away from the cave mouth towards him.

"How many cops you got here?" Rooke asked.

"Just Ryan. He's inside somewhere. They must've taken his gun."

"Can I use yours?" Rooke asked.

"No worries, just uncuff me first. Keys are on my belt. See 'em?"

"Yeah, I see 'em," said Rooke, pulling the key off the clip and the gun from the belt. He unlocked the cuffs, and as Watson turned around and opened his mouth to speak, Rooke shot him in the eye, killing him instantly.

"Shit," Rooke said, his face speckled with Watson's blood. He wiped it off and held up the rifle, looking through the night-vision scope. He took a lint cloth from his pocket and wiped the specks of blood from the lens.

***

Rooke peered inside the cave with the scope. He saw Ryan

lying dead on the balcony. A few steps from him was the old man, slouched on the balcony with his back against the wall, eyes closed. No sign of anyone else. Was the lawyer hauling ass through the cave, or waiting for him to walk in? Keeping perfectly still, he listened. Not a sound. The lawyer was in a panic and had run up to the balcony only a minute or so earlier. If he were in the chamber, Rooke would have heard him breathing. But he didn't. He looked over the chamber with the scope once more, then stepped inside. If the lawyer was going to shoot, it would be at that moment. Still silence. He walked up the passage to Ryan and knew immediately he was dead. He stepped over to the old man, looked him over. Fatal chest wound, massive bleeding; another corpse. Rooke looked down the passage and saw a faint, shimmering light reflecting off a wall. Then it was gone.

Abe swung the nulla-nulla with great speed, connecting with Rooke's ankle, sending him to the floor. Abe tried to choke him, got a grip of his windpipe, but Rooke was highly trained for such scenarios and immediately freed himself and had the old man in a wrist lock. Rooke got to his feet and planted a foot hard on the side of Abe's chest opposite the bullet wound. He thrust down, forcing the blood to pump from the wound, Abe groaning. Rooke thrust harder, pumping, intent on bleeding out the old man quickly.

***

Tom followed David along the natural passage that led

through the depths of the cave, climbing over boulders and weaving through narrow passages. The air was thinner and it was harder to breathe for both of them. David stopped and reached inside a small nook, pulling out a spear. Tom could hear water flowing nearby.

"That's it," David said, shining the light to a natural doorway. "That's our way out."

They walked through the arching doorway into the chamber, where the sound of flowing water was much louder. Jagged rock walls, blood red in colour, twisted and converged way up to a black void above. David led Tom down a sloping, smooth floor to the far end, where water poured from a spring and flowed beneath a wall of rock.

"It'll take us out to the river," David said.

"Under that wall?" Tom said, noticing that there was no head room between the stream and the rock above it. David nodded and stepped into the knee-deep water. "How long do we have to hold our breaths?"

"I don't know."

"So you haven't done this before?"

"No."

"Give me the flashlight for a minute," Tom said. David handed it over and Tom looked around the cave. He spotted a tall, narrow passage. "How about this? Is this another way out?"

"No."

Tom soon found another passage and approached the entrance, shining the torch inside. The passage curved into darkness, the walls lined with nooks and alcoves. Tom turned back to David. "How about this one?"

"There's no . . ." David froze, terror in his eyes.

Tom turned and saw Tracker Jackson leaning out from the passage, eyes and mouth wide open, a wooden club held above his head. Tom ducked backwards, but not in time to evade the blow, which sent him to the floor. Out cold. The flashlight was still in Tom's hand, lighting up a good portion of the chamber.

David leapt from the water, spear poised. He and Tracker circled each other like a couple of boxers, neither one wanting to strike first for fear of missing and leaving themselves open. David's eyes were fixed on the man he had thought was his father. The man who betrayed him and his grandfather; who wanted him dead.

They circled around for what seemed like a long time. Tracker was too close, and David thought that if he drew the spear back, Tracker would strike before he could release it. He needed a little more space to keep Tracker out of striking distance and stepped backwards. Tracker advanced, not allowing David to widen the space between them.

His pulse thumping in his throat, David jumped backwards, then realised that he had been corralled into the passage Tracker had come from. Tracker pounced forward, and David hustled back even deeper into the passage, then drew the spear back. Tracker stepped sideways, out of view.

Spear ready, eyes wide open, David waited. Then he felt something closing in all around him: a net made of vine. Tracker stepped into view, pulling on a single cord of vine which tightened the net and trapped David like an animal.

"Gotcha!" Tracker said, heaving on the net and bringing David to ground with a thump. David squirmed, trying to find a way out as Tracker dragged him out onto the chamber floor.

He struggled desperately, wriggling and twisting his body, which only seemed to make the net tighten. He tried to break the vine but it was as tough as rope. He stopped struggling and looked up to see Tracker standing over him.

"Close your eyes, boy, and I'll make it quick," he said, and raised the club above his head to strike a deadly blow.

But he became aware of something behind him, and he whipped around on his heels to see Rooke standing inside the entrance, rifle in hand. Tracker raised a hand just before a deafening shot was fired. He growled in pain as the bullet split his hand between the middle fingers and grazed his neck.

Tracker hurled the club at Rooke, knocking the rifle from his hands, then charged him, the two of them going to ground.

David struggled to free himself as Rooke and Tracker assaulted each other with elbows, knees, fists and foreheads, blood streaming. Tracker had a significant size and weight advantage and managed to lay a chokehold that Rooke couldn't break.

David pulled on various threads of vine, one after another, until finally he found the release thread. He wound it in and an opening appeared over his chest. He kept winding until it was as wide as his shoulders, then scrambled free. He dashed back to the passage and grabbed the spear. He glanced at Tom, still unconscious, a bloody wound on the side of his head. But at least he was breathing.

David stalked towards the two men as they fought to the death in the centre of the chamber floor. He decided he would wait till it was over and then kill the victor, before they killed him. It looked like it was going to be Tracker.

Rooke, veins almost bursting from his temples, reached towards his ankle. David held the spear ready, aiming for the centre of Tracker's back. He saw Rooke's eyes flutter as he approached unconsciousness. David took a deep breath and gritted his teeth.

Then, a muffled gunshot. Tracker groaned. The second shot, unmuffled and much louder than the first, woke Tom.

Tracker slumped on top of Rooke, forcing him onto his back. They both lay still, and David approached, spear drawn. He could hear Rooke gasping for breath, but he couldn't see him pointing the gun over Tracker's shoulder, waiting for a clean shot.

Tom rolled onto his side, and he saw Rooke, gun in hand, pinned under Tracker's body, preparing to shoot David, who was slowly circling around Tracker.

Tom spotted the police handgun on the floor nearby. He reached for it as Rooke sat up to shoot the boy.

David hurled the spear, splitting Rooke's chest open as Rooke recoiled in pain, firing harmlessly into the cave wall. He lay on his back, coughing up blood. David approached cautiously. Rooke raised the gun again, but

Tom fired first, unloading a deadly barrage of bullets into the side of Rooke's head, neck and torso. Rooke lay still on the floor, the spear sticking straight up from his chest.

David checked Tracker for a pulse. He didn't have one. He rolled Tracker onto his back and looked into the dead eyes of the man he had always feared.

"Let's go, Tom," David said, gesturing to the stream.

"I think we can walk out the way we came in. Pretty sure they're all dead now."

David frowned, then gasped in realisation and bolted out of the chamber.

Tom picked up the flashlight and staggered after him, nursing a gash on the side of his forehead. He walked up through the winding passage and finally came to the balcony, where David was sitting with Abe's lifeless body in his arms, squeezing as if to force the life back into him. Tom gave David some space and sat down on the cave floor, back against the wall.

Chapter 35

In the centre lobby of the Old Pearl Hotel, Claire stood at a podium before a crowd of reporters, cameras and microphones.

"It's been a tremendous honour to serve this great state of ours, and we trust that you'll re-elect us to continue our important work."

There was a sudden commotion at the far side of the room. Claire tried to ignore it.

"We've already achieved so much, including—" She stopped, the noise too loud to ignore. She turned to the far side of the room and looked in horror to see her face projected on the wall. The reporters and camera operators around her began to flock to the projection, and she watched in stunned silence as the video Tom had recorded in her hotel room was being played.

"I swear, I had no knowledge of any kidnapping," Claire said on the screen.

"You must've had an inkling," Tom said.

"I leave that kind of thing to Drake. She makes things happen, I don't ask how. When things need to be done . . ."

"What? You step aside?"

"There are powerful people. You have no idea."

Claire collapsed to the floor and two bodyguards raced to her aid. Drake stormed over to the crowd and saw the young journalist at the centre, operating the phone and projector as the incriminating drama on the screen continued.

"Families who've been in the party for generations . . ." Claire said.

"Turn that device off now!" Drake yelled. But Hannah ignored her, and the journalists and camera crew continued to record and broadcast. "Let me through! I demand that you let me through!" Drake said.

"Shut up! This is important!" a journalist yelled back at her.

She tried to barge her way through to the projector, but the reporters kept her at bay as the video continued.

"They're like dynasties of power brokers. You hardly ever see them, but they . . . I mean, I'm free to lead the party, but if I stray from their agenda, they 'correct' things. They make things . . ."

"Happen? Disappear?" Tom asked.

"Security!" Drake yelled. One of the bodyguards was carrying Claire to the elevators while the other ran to Drake's side.

> *"A child, Claire. They're going to murder a child!" Tom said on the screen. Claire turned away from him.*

"Get that phone and projector!" Drake told the bodyguard. He shoved his way through the crowd, and some of the cameras turned on him. He looked up to the screen and saw himself and his colleague beating up Tom. He froze for a moment, then lunged, grabbing the projector and phone.

"Don't worry, we got enough of it!" someone yelled to Claire.

"It went out already, live broadcast!" someone else yelled.

The bodyguard returned to Drake's side and a journalist recognised her from the video.

"It's her!" and stepped between them, putting a microphone in Drake's face. "How do you respond to the video you just saw?"

Drake began to silently panic as all the cameras and microphones began to turn towards her, questions coming from all sides.

"Do you control the Premier?"

"Who are the dynasties of power brokers?"

The blood drained from Drake's face as she stared at the

cameras for a moment before fleeing for the elevator.

Chapter 36

David wiped his eyes and sniffed as he and Tom walked out of the cave into the early morning sun. The boy looked up and took a deep breath; then he and Tom walked down the hill towards the parked police car.

The sound of the approaching vehicle sent both of them ducking out of sight. Tom pulled the Glock out from under his belt and peered over the hood of the parked car to see another police car swinging around the bend and into the clearing. Kris was at the wheel.

"She's all right," Tom said, nodding at David to reassure him.

Kris parked beside them and got out, immediately noticing the pair of them were covered in scratches and dried blood, and Tom's face was battered.

"Are you both okay?" Tom and David looked at each other, then nodded in agreement.

"How about you? Looks like you had a rough night."

"I'm okay," she said, and looked up at the cave. "So what happened?"

"They're dead. All of 'em," David said.

She was taken aback and didn't quite know how to respond. She noticed how dry they both looked and handed David the water bottle from her belt. He took a few good swallows and handed it to Tom.

"Hop in the car," she said.

"Nah, I'm okay."

"It's gonna be a scorcher, mate. You don't want to walk all the way back in this heat," Tom said.

"Gonna rain soon," David said.

"I need to take you into the station," Kris said. "You'll have to make a statement."

"No way," David said.

"I know it's the last thing—"

"I'll take care of the statements and anything else, as his legal representative," Tom said.

"Is that all right with you, David?" Kris asked.

David looked up at Tom, squinting in the sun. Then he smiled broadly. "How much you charge?"

"It's pro bono."

"Hey?"

"My shout," Tom said.

David nodded. "Yeah, that's okay. He can be my lawyer."

"We better shake on it," Tom said, offering his hand. David shook it. "You sure we can't give you a ride? It's a bloody long walk."

"Well, I got plenty of walking to do. You know what I mean?"

"Yeah, I know," Tom said. David slapped him gently on the back, and they stepped away from each other.

"I'll come see you soon," Tom said.

"Come any time, mate," David said. Then he turned and began walking through the scrub.

Kris put her hands on Tom's forearms. "You sure you're okay?"

He nodded and noticed scratch marks on her throat.

"You got hurt."

She shook her head.

"I guess you won the fight," he said. She smiled and nodded. Tom hugged her and she hugged him back.

He turned back to David, still walking further away. Kris held open the passenger door and Tom sat inside. He was still watching David as she turned the vehicle around and headed down the hill.

***

David walked through the vast wilderness; rich, red earth, sunburnt scrub and towering, blood red boulders, iridescent in the morning sun. He heard the distant sound of feet rustling through spinifex and turned to see Tom running through the scrub towards him. He smiled and stood waiting as Tom jumped over bushes and nearly stumbled, but managed to keep his feet. Soon, he was by David's side, and they set off together.

A word from the author

Thank you for reading *Outback Creed.* If you enjoyed it, please leave a review on Amazon. Just a sentence or two could really make a difference in helping other readers find this book.

For a free copy of my thriller, *Prior Violations,* visit:

http://www.jonthanmacpherson.com/

Follow me:

Facebook
http://www.facebook.com/jonathanmacpherson.author/

Instagram
http://www.instagram.com/macpherson.jonathan/

Brazen Violations

"Move, damn it!" Detective Betts yelled at the station wagon ahead of him as it cruised along like the driver was taking in the sights of suburbia. There was a little shaving cream smeared on the top of his collar and on the underside of his jaw, and his shirt was untucked. His jacket and holstered gun sat on the passenger seat. He had left home in a hurry.

He hit a button and blue police lights flashed from the dashboard, accompanied by a loud burst of siren. The station wagon pulled to the roadside and Betts put his foot down, charging ahead, his hands clamped on the wheel.

Without braking, he turned into a narrow alley, sweat dripping from his forehead, rippling down over wrinkle lines and into his eyes, forcing him to blink.

He noticed the black sedan in the rear-view mirror, gaining on him. He accelerated but it continued to close in, two car lengths behind him now, its occupants hidden by tinted windows.

The one-way alley was tight, lined on both sides by

garages and the back fences of houses. It curved into a blind turn and he took it at speed, then immediately hit the brakes, seeing the van parked in front of him. The black sedan stopped behind him and he recognized he was being ambushed. He whipped out the handgun, hyper-alert now, but at the same time calm in a way that only comes with training and experience.

Eyes darting from the mirrors to the van in front, he tried the door, but it wouldn't open more than a few inches, hemmed in by a back fence. He reached for the passenger door but flinched as the business end of a crowbar burst through the window, shattering the glass and barely missing his face. It recoiled and Betts looked up to see two ski-masked guys leaning over the fence, one of them tossing a canister onto the floor, passenger side, gas pouring out of it. Betts thrust his gun up and took aim but the masked men ducked out of sight. He fired a couple of shots into the fence then grabbed the canister and tossed it out the window. But it was too late, the car was already filled with the stuff. With a hand over his mouth, he turned and fired through the back window at the car behind him, his bullets bouncing off the bullet-proof windshield of the sedan. Betts held his aim, waiting for someone to get out of the vehicle. Then his vision began to blur. He shook his head, then felt himself sliding down the seat as he lost consciousness. He fired some more, emptying the gun as he slid onto his back on the passenger seat. A blurry, ski-masked head leaned through the window, hovering above Betts, inspecting him, just before he blacked out.

***

The darkness was heavy and all around him, smothering him entirely so he couldn't move a finger or a toe, couldn't open his eyes. There was no sound except for his breathing, labored and deep.

Then he felt something. A slight stinging, so faint it seemed far above him. But it was definitely a stinging and he noticed that it was accompanied by a high-pitched noise, like a dental drill. The stinging and the noise intensified, building as he returned to consciousness.

Detective Betts lay on his back squinting his bloodshot eyes. Three blurred figures were leaning over him, fixated on his chest where one of them was holding something, doing something. It was painful. He soon realized they were performing surgery. His first thought was that he must have been shot and brought to a hospital. Then he noticed the thrash metal music screaming on a stereo nearby, and the air thick with cigar smoke, bitter in his nose and mouth. This was no hospital.

As his vision improved he noticed one of the figures was a broadly shouldered, middle-aged woman with a face that was once attractive, but now bore jagged scars from a violent past. She puffed on the cigar as a younger man, heavy and stinking of cologne, used a handkerchief to wipe the pouring sweat off the surgeon's face. With wild, unkempt grey hair and gritted teeth, the surgeon carved into Betts' chest with a whirring electronic tool, holding it like a dagger.

Betts felt a sobering surge of adrenalin and his left arm sprung out, clutching the surgeon's hand. With his right, he went for the throat, grabbed it, squeezing as hard as he could. The surgeon struggled, trying to pull free. Betts leant closer to get a better grip, but the younger guy shoved a rag over his face. He thrashed about like a fish on a hook, unable to get the thing off his face. The chloroform, sweet and strong, sent him straight back to unconsciousness.

***

End of Excerpt.

Made in the USA
Monee, IL
14 June 2022

98016076R00132